PRAISE FOR NOT THIS AUGUST:

"Kornbluth was as good at giving us surprising insights that illuminate the world we live in as any other author who lived. NOT THIS AUGUST is . . . witty, powerful, and illuminating."

— Frederik Pohl

"Suddenly, news of the surrender of our last big ground force to the nation by the President. A few hours later the President and Vice President were shot as war criminals . . . So begins a novel we think you'll find hard to put down once you've started it . . . a far more powerful effect on the American readers than George Orwell's *1984* . . . He did it with masterly skill . . . We hope that it may have the widest possible circulation . . . a grim warning of what Americans have to look forward to if they let down the national guard as long as world Communism remains on the prowl.

PS: For the benefit of those who can't take stark, unrelieved tragedy, we'll say that this book has an ending which is not too unhappy; but you'd better read NOT THIS AUGUST to find out what that ending is."

— The Sunday Edition of
The New York *Daily News*

"Better than all the rest."
— *Kirkus*

C. M. KORNBLUTH

Revised and with a
Foreword and Afterword by Frederik Pohl

TOR

A TOM DOHERTY ASSOCIATES BOOK

NOT THIS AUGUST

Copyright © 1955 by C. M. Kornbluth

First Tor printing: December 1981
Second printing: November 1986

A TOR Book

Published by Tom Doherty Associates, Inc.
49 West 24 Street
New York, N.Y. 10010

Cover art by Tom Kidd

ISBN: 0-812-54318-1
CAN. ED.: 0-812-54319-X

Printed in the United States of America

0 9 8 7 6 5 4 3 2 1

NOT

THIS

AUGUST

Introduction:
NOT THIS AUGUST

FREDERIK POHL

In the mid-1950s, *The New York Sunday News* had close to the largest circulation of any newspaper in the world. It was, accordingly, edited for a lowest common denominator of taste and sophistication. Lots of sports. Lots of pictures. Lots of short, simple sentences, with lots of one-syllable words. The *News* paid little attention to books, least of all to science-fiction books. Nevertheless, on August 14th, 1955, *News* readers opening to the editorial page were confronted with a photograph of a science-fiction writer named C.M. Kornbluth, and a full-length lead editorial devoted entirely to "a new novel which we think you'll find hard to put down once you've started it: 'Not This

August,' by C.M. Kornbluth . . . . We hope that it may have the widest possible circulation." The editorial is unsigned, but whoever wrote it obviously liked the book; the column is sprinkled with phrases like "masterly skill" and compares *Not This August* with *1984*—to the disadvantage of *1984*.

As far as I know, the *News* has never since given so much attention to a science-fiction novel, and of course it took an unusual sort of science-fiction novel to bring it about then. *Not This August* is cautionary science fiction, in the great tradition of *1984*—and of *Brave New World*, *On the Beach* and many others. It is not meant as prediction. It is only meant as a warning. It doesn't say what will happen, positively, but what *may* happen, *if*—

Not This August was first published a quarter of a century ago and, until this new edition was in preparation, I had not read it since it first came out. I didn't know if it would stand up after all those years; but when I took it up again it gripped me from the first page, and kept me turning pages until the end, and left me wishing for more when it was done. History did not go the way Cyril Kornbluth outlined in this book when he was writing in the gritty, mean 1950s. But the essence of the novel is still true.

Reading this novel about a future that might have happened, but didn't, leaves a bittersweet taste in my mouth. Cyril Kornbluth was my close friend, valued collaborator and esteemed author of a disproportionate share of the best science fiction being written in the years around 1950. The bitterness rises from the fact that his career came to an abrupt end not long after *Not This August* appeared. When Cyril was twenty he went off to fight in World War II. He carried a 50-caliber heavy machine-gun around the battle of the Ardennes Forest and did himself permanent harm. His heart was stretched past its capacity to heal, and in 1958 he died of it. I think he might have lived to be the greatest of us all, because he was certainly heading in that direction. But when he died— at the age of 34!—he left a handful of books of his own, a few more written in collaboration with Judith Merril or with me, a few dozen short stories and novelettes—and a lasting regret. He was just beginning to hit his stride.

Cyril Kornbluth was born in New York City in 1923, narrowly escaped crib death in his first year, at the age of five was rescued by his brother while attempting to make revolver cartridges go bang with a hammer, and then, while still a high-school student, discovered the world of science fiction. We met when Cyril became a member of the New York Futurians, the sf-fan-cum would-be writer group that produced Isaac Asimov, James Blish, Damon Knight and a good many others who made a mark in science fiction. Cyril was probably the youngest Futurian in 1938, and very likely the most talented: short, plump, unathletic, cynical, he fit right in.

Cyril was one of the brightest people I have ever known, but not much of that quick intelligence showed up academically. At fifteen, he was already beginning to write. By sixteen he was beginning to sell, and likely enough he could not see much relevance in what he was studying in George Washington High School to the life of a novelist that was beginning to seem possible. Likely enough he was right. Novelists need to know a great many things, but not very many of them are taught in schools. One teacher made an impression. Her name was Mary J. J. Wrinn, a poet herself, who had published a text on poetry called *The Golden Treasury.* Cyril carried the book around to read on the long subway trips from Inwood, last Manhattan outpost south of the Bronx, to Flatbush, where the Futurians usually met in Brooklyn, and when I saw it I begged to borrow it. It described every formal verse form, from the sestina to the chant royale, and for a month or two Cyril and I competed in writing sonnets and villanelles—an exercise I still recommend to any would-be writer. It was Mary Wrinn's hope that Cyril would become a major poet, and I think it might have happened if he had not preferred science fiction. Partly economics were involved. Cyril's father was a Civil Service court attendant. It was a good job and a responsible one, but not calculated to create a family fortune. It was clear to Cyril that whatever he did with his life he would have to support himself at it. In those terms, science fiction held a more promising future. (Considering the minute space rates science-fiction writers earned in the 1930s, think of how much that says about the lot of the poet!)

At any rate, Cyril's grades were not distinguished, by the standards of George Washington High School. In his senior year he applied for entrance to City College and was turned down because of his grades. His father diagnosed the situation easily enough—not lack of ability, simple lack of incentive—and so he offered Cyril $5 to take a special entrance examination and pass it, which, of course, Cyril did with ease. Cyril's school record was not nearly as impressive as that of his straight-A schoolmate, young Heinz Kissinger—but all Kissinger grew up to be was Secretary of State.

In preparing *Not This August* for its new publication I have taken the liberty of making a few textual changes. This is not done to deceive, only to eliminate some jarring anachronisms. What the book has to say is unchanged.

One could object to *Not This August* as a failed prediction, but of course it was never meant that way. That is one of the great virtues of cautionary science fiction. The story need not come true to be valuable—in fact, no one wants it to come true, the author least of all. What Cyril Kornbluth wanted us to know when he wrote *Not This August* was that there were grave dangers in the world—there still are, and much the same dangers; and that averting or rectifying those dangers presented graver dangers still, as the ending shows. And those, too, are unfortunately still present, and still need to be guarded against.

But it is not for the heuristic and normative values of science fiction that most people read it—thank heaven! We read it for fun, especially for the ironical, surprising insights that illuminate the world we live in.

Cyril Kornbluth was about as good at giving us those startling insights as any science-fiction writer who ever lived. *Not This August* is vintage Kornbluth—witty, powerful and illuminating—and I am more pleased than I can say to see it available once more.

—Frederik Pohl

"Not this August, nor this September; you have this year to do what you like. Not next August, nor next September; that is still too soon . . . But the year after that or the year after that they fight."

Ernest Hemingway
Notes on the Next War

BOOK 1

CHAPTER ONE

The blackest day in the history of the United States started like any other day for Billy Justin. Thirty-seven years old, once a free-lance commercial artist, a pensioned veteran of Korea, he was now a dairy farmer, and had been during the three years of the war. It was that or be drafted to a road crew—with great luck, a factory bench.

He rose, therefore, at five-fifteen, shut off his alarm clock, and went, bleary-eyed, in bathrobe and slippers, to milk his eight cows. He hefted the milk cans to the platform for the pickup truck of the Eastern Milkshed Administration and briefly considered washing out the milking machine and pails as he ought to. He then gave a disgusted look at his barn, his house, his fields—the things that once were supposed to afford him a decent, dignified retirement and had become instead vampires of his leisure—and shambled back to bed.

At the more urbane hour of ten he *really* got up and had breakfast, including an illegal egg withheld from his quota. Over unspeakably synthetic coffee he consulted the electricity bulletin tacked to his kitchen wall and sourly muttered: "Goody." Today was the day Chiunga County rural residents got four hours of juice—ten-thirty to two-thirty.

The most important item was recharging his car battery. He vaguely understood that it ruined batteries to just stand when they were run down. Still in bathrobe and slippers he went to his sagging garage, unbolted the corroded battery terminals, and clipped on the leads from the trickle charger that hung on the wall. Not that four hours of trickle would do a lot of good, he reflected, but maybe he could scrounge some tractor gas somewhere. Old man Croley down in the store at Norton was supposed to have an arrangement with the Liquid Fuels Administration tank-truck driver.

Ten-thirty struck while he was still in the garage; he saw the needle on the charger dial kick over hard and heard a buzz. So *that* was all right.

Quite a few lights were on in the house. The last allotment of juice had come in late afternoon and evening, which made considerably more sense than ten-thirty to two-thirty. Chiunga County, he decided after reflection, was getting the short end as usual.

The radio, ancient and slow to warm up, boomed at him suddenly: " . . . bring you all in your time of trial and striving, the Hour of Faith. Beloved sisters and brethren, let us pray. Almighty Father—"

Justin said without rancor, "Amen," and turned the dial to the other CONELRAD station. Early in the war that used to be one of the biggest of the nuisances: only two broadcast frequencies allowed instead of the old American free-for-all which would have guided bombers or missiles. With only two frequencies you had, of course, only two programs, and frequently both of them stank. It was surprising how easily you forgot the early pique when Current Conversation went through and you rarely heard the programs.

He was pleased to find a newscast on the other channel.

"The Defense Department announced today that the fighting south of El Paso continues to rage. Soviet units have penetrated to within three hundred yards of the American defense perimeter. Canadian armored forces are hammering at the flanks of their salient in a determined attack involving hundreds of Acheson tanks and 280-millimeter self-propelled cannon. The morale of our troops continues high and individual acts of heroism are too numerous to describe here.

"Figures released today indicate that the enemy on the home front is being as severely and as justly dealt with as the foreign invader to whom he pledges allegiance. A terse announcement from Lewisburg Federal Penitentiary included this report: 'Civilians executed for treason during the six-month period just ending—784.' From this reporter to the FBI, a hearty 'Well done!'

"The Attorney General's office issued a grim and pointed warning today that the Harboring of Deserters Act means precisely what it says and will be enforced to the letter. The government will seek the death penalty against eighty-seven-year-old Mrs. Arthur Schwartz of Chicago, who allegedly gave money and food to her grandson, Private William O. Temple, as he was passing through Chicago after deserting under fire from the United States Army. Temple, of course, was apprehended in Windsor, Ontario, on March 17 and shot.

"Good news for candy lovers! The Nonessential Foodstuffs Agency reports that a new substitute chocolate has passed testing and will soon be available to B-card holders at all groceries. It's just two points for a big, big, half-ounce bar! From this reporter to the hard-working boys and girls of the NFA, a hearty—"

Justin, a little nauseated, snapped the set off. It was time to walk up to his mailbox anyway. He hoped to hitch a ride on into Norton with the postwoman. The connecting rod of his well pump had broken and he was getting sick of hoisting up his water with a bucket. Old man Croley might have a rod or know somebody who'd make him one.

He dressed quickly and sloppily, and didn't even think of shaving. "How are you fixed for blades?" wasn't much of a joke by then. He puffed up the steep quarter mile to his box and leaned on it, scanning the winding blacktop to the north, from which she would come. He understood that a new girl had been carrying the mail for ten days or so and wondered what had happened to Mrs. Elkins —fat, friendly, unkempt Mrs. Elkins, who couldn't add and whose mailbox notes in connection with postage due and stamps and money orders purchased were marvels of illegibility and confusion. He hadn't seen the new girl yet, nor had there been any occasion for notes between them.

Deep in the cloudless blue sky to the north there was a sudden streak of white scribbled across heaven—condensation trail of a stratosphere guided missile. The wild jogs and jolts meant it was set for evasive action. Not very interested, he decided that it must be a Soviet job trying just once more for the optical and instrument shops of Corning, or possibly the fair-sized air force base at Elmira. Launched, no doubt, from a Russian or Chinese submarine somewhere in the Atlantic. But as he watched, Continental Air Defense came through again. It almost always did. Half a dozen thinner streaks of white soared vertically from nowhere, bracketed the bogey, and then there was a golden glint of light up there that meant mission accomplished. Those CAD girls were *good*, he appreciatively thought. Cruise missiles, stratospheric missiles, if they were within the air the girls got them, and if they weren't the antiballistic lasers picked them off from orbit. Too bad about Chicago and Pittsburgh, but the girls were green then . . . Of course, if the Reds had had anti-radar ghosts it would have been all over. But they hadn't. And once the U.S. got its own ghost satellite going—

It wasn't going yet, though; and the fighting was closer every day to where it waited for launch.

It did not pay to think such thoughts.

He shaded his eyes to look down the black-top again. What he saw made him blink incredulously. A kiddie-car going faster than a kiddie-car should—or a magnified roller skate—but with two flailing pistons—

The preposterous vehicle closed up to him and creaked to a stop, and was suddenly no longer preposterous. It was a neatly made three-wheel wagon steered by a tiller bar on the front wheel. The power was supplied by a man in khaki who alternately pushed two levers connected to a crankshaft, which was also the rear axle of the cart. The man had no legs below his thighs.

He said cheerfully to Justin: "Need a farm-hand, mister?"

Justin, manners completely forgotten, could only stare.

The man said: "I get around in this thing all right and it gives me shoulders like a bull. Be surprised what I can do. String fence, run a tractor if you're lucky, ride a horse if you ain't, milk, cut wood, housework—and besides, who else can you get, mister?"

He took out a hunk of dense, homemade bread and began to chew on it.

Justin said slowly: "I know what you mean, and I'd be very happy to hire you if I could, but I can't. I'm just snake-hipping through the Farm-or-Fight Law with eight cows. I haven't got pasture for more and I can't buy grain, of course. There just isn't work for another pair of hands or food for another mouth."

"I see," the man said agreeably. "There anybody around here who might take me on?"

"Try the Shiptons," Justin said. "Down this road, third house on the left. It used to be white with green shutters. About two miles. They're always moaning about they need help and can't get it."

"Thanks a lot, mister. I'll call their bluff. Would you mind giving me a push off? This thing starts hard for all it runs good once it's going."

"Wait a minute," Justin said almost angrily. "Do you have to do this? I mean, I tremendously admire your spirit, but Goddamn it, the country's supposed to see that you fellows don't have to break your backs on a farm!"

"Spirit hell," the man grinned. "No offense, but you farmers just don't *know*."

"Isn't your pension adequate? My God, it should be. For *that*."

"It's adequate," the man said. "Three hundred a month—more'n I ever made in my life. But I got good and sick of the trouble collecting it. Skipped months, get somebody else's check, get the check but they forgot to sign it. And when you get the right check with the right amount and signed right, you got four-five days' wait at the bank standing in line. I figured it out and wrote 'em they could cut me to a hundred so long as they paid it in silver dollars. Got back a letter saying my bid for twenty-five gross of chrome-steel forgings was satisfactory and a contract letter would be forthcoming. I just figured things are pretty bad, they *might* get worse, and I want to be on a farm when they do, if they do. No offense, as I say, but you people don't know how good you have it. No cholera up here for instance, is there?"

"Cholera? Good God, no!"

"There—you see? Mind pushing me off now, mister? It's hot just sitting here."

Justin pushed him off. He went twinkling down the road, left-hand-right-hand-left-hand-right—

Cholera?

He hadn't even asked the man where. New York? Boston? But he got the Sunday *Times* every week—

The postwoman drove up in a battered Buick. She was young and pretty, and she was obviously scared stiff to find a strange unshaven man waiting for her at a stop.

"I'm Billy Justin," he hastily explained through the window lowered a crack. "One of your best customers, even if I did forget to shave. Anything for me today?"

She poked his copy of the *Times* through the crack, smiled nervously, and shifted preparatory to starting.

"Please," he said, "I was wondering if you'd do me a considerable favor. Drive me in to Norton?"

"I was told not to," she said. "Deserters, shirkers—you never know."

"Ma'am," he said, "I'm an honest dairyman, redeemed by the Farm-or-Fight Law from a life of lucrative shame as a commercial artist. All I have to offer is gratitude and my sincere assurance that I wouldn't bother you if I could possibly make it there and back on foot in time for the milking."

"Commercial artist?" she asked. "Well, I suppose it's all right." She smiled and opened the door.

It was four miles to Norton, with a stop at every farmhouse. It took an hour. He found out that her name was Betsy Cardew. She was twenty. She had been studying physics at Cornell, which exempted her from service except for R.W.O.T.C. courses.

"Why not admit it?" She shrugged. "I flunked out. It was nonsense my tackling physics in the first place, but my father insisted. Well, he found out he couldn't buy brains for me, so here I am."

She seemed to regard "here"—in the driver's seat of a rural free delivery car, one of the cushiest jobs going—as a degrading, uncomfortable place.

He snapped his fingers. "Cardew," he said. "T.C.?"

"That's my pop."

And that explained why Betsy wasn't in the

WAC or the CAD or a labor battalion sewing shirts for soldiers. T. C. Cardew lived in a colonial mansion on a hill, and he was a National Committeeman. He shopped in Scranton or New York but he owned the ground on which almost every store in Chiunga County stood.

"Betsy," he said tentatively, "we haven't known each other very long, but I have come to regard you with reverent affection. I feel toward you as a brother. Don't you think it would be nice of Mr. T. C. Cardew adopted me to make it legal?"

She laughed sharply. "It's nice to hear a joke again," she said. "But frankly you wouldn't like it. To be blunt, Mr. T. C. Cardew is a skunk. I had a nice mother once, but he divorced her."

He was considerably embarrassed. After a pause he asked: "You been in any of the big cities lately? New York, Boston?"

"Boston last month. My plane from Ithaca got forced into the northbound traffic pattern and the pilot didn't dare turn. We would've gone down on the CAD screen as a bogey, and *wham*. The ladies don't ask questions first any more. Not since Chicago and Pittsburgh."

"How was Boston?"

"I just saw the airport. The usual thing— beggars, wounded, garbage in the streets. No flies—too early in the year."

"I have a feeling that we in the country don't know what's going on outside our own little milk routes. I also have a feeling that the folks in Boston don't know about the folks in

New York and vice versa."

"Mr. Justin, your feeling is well grounded," she said emphatically. "The big cities are hellholes because conditions have become absolutely unbearable and still people have to bear them. Did you know New York's under martial law?"

"No!"

"Yes. The 104th Division and the 33rd Armored Division are in town. They're needed in El Paso, but they were yanked North to keep New York from going through with a secession election."

He almost said something stupid ("I didn't read about it in the *Times*") but caught himself. She went on: "Of course, I shouldn't be telling you state secrets, but I've noticed at home that a state secret is something known to everybody who makes more than fifty thousand a year and to nobody who makes less. Don't you feel rich now, Mr. Justin?"

"Filthy rich. Don't worry, by the way. I won't pass anything on to anybody."

"Bless you, I know that! Your mail's read, your phone's monitored, and your neighbors are probably itching to collect a bounty on you for turning you in as a D-or-S." A "D-or-S" was a "disaffected or seditious person"—not quite a criminal and certainly not a full-fledged citizen. He usually found himself making camouflage nets behind barbed wire in Nevada, never fully realizing what had hit him.

"You're a little rough on my neighbors. Nobody gets turned in around here for shooting off his mouth. It's still a small corner of America."

Insanely dangerous to be talking like that to a stranger—insanely dangerous and wildly exhilarating. Sometimes he hiked over to the truck farm of his friends the Bradens, also city exiles, and they had sessions into the small hours that cleared their minds of gripes intolerably accumulated like pus in a boil. Amy Braden's powerful home brew helped . . . .

Rumble-rumble, they rolled over the Lehigh's tracks at the Norton grade crossing; Croley's store was dead ahead at the end of the short main street. Norton, New York, had a population of about sixty old people and no young ones. Since a few brief years of glory a century and a half ago as a major riverboat town on the Susquehanna it had been running down. But somehow Croley made a store there pay.

She parked neatly and handed him a big sheaf of mail. "Give these to the Great Stone Face," she said. "I don't like to look at him."

"Thanks for the ride," he said. "And the talk."

She flashed a smile. "We must do it more often," and drove away.

Immediately, thinking of his return trip, he canvassed the cars and wagons lined up before Croley's. When he recognized Gus Feinblatt's stake wagon drawn by Tony and Phony, the two big geldings, he knew he had it made. Gus was that fantastic rarity, a Jewish farmer, and he lived up the road from Justin.

The store was crowded down to the tip of its ell. Everybody in Norton was there, standing packed in utter silence. Croley's grim face swiveled toward him as he entered; then the storekeeper nodded at a freezer compartment where he could sit.

Justin wanted to yell: "What is this, a gag?"

Then the radio, high on a shelf, spoke. As it spoke, Justin realized that it had been saying the same thing for possibly half an hour, over and over again, but that people stayed and listened to it over and over again, numbly waiting for somebody to cry "Hoax" or "Get away from that mike you dirty Red" or anything but what it would say.

The radio said: "Ladies and gentlemen, the President of the United States." Then the inimitable voice, but weary, deathly weary. "My fellow Americans. Our armed forces have met with terrible defeat on land and at sea. I have just been advised by General Fraley that he has unconditionally surrendered the Army of the Southwest to Generals Novikov and Feng. General Fraley said the only choice before him was surrender or the annihilation of his troops to the last man by overwhelmingly superior forces. History must judge the wisdom of his choice; here and now I can only say that his capitulation removes the last barrier to the northward advance of the armies of the Soviet Union and the Chinese People's Republic.

"My fellow citizens, I must now tell you that for three months the United States has not possessed a fleet in being. It was destroyed in a great air-sea battle off the Azores, a battle whose results it was thought wisest to conceal temporarily.

"We are disarmed. We are defeated.

"I have by now formally communicated the capitulation of the United States of America to the U.S.S.R. and the C.P.R. to our embassy in Switzerland, where it will be handed to the Russian and Chinese embassies.

"As Commander-in-Chief of the Armed Forces of the United States I now order all officers and enlisted men and women to cease fire. Maintain discipline, hold your ranks, but offer no opposition to the advance of the invading armies, for resistance would be a futile waste of lives—and an offense for which the invading armies might retaliate tenfold. You will soon be returned to your homes and families in an orderly demobilization. Until then maintain discipline. You were a great fighting force, but you were outnumbered.

"To the civilians of the United States I also say 'Maintain discipline.' Your task is the harder, for it must be self-discipline. Keep order. Obey the laws of the land. Respect authority. Make no foolish demonstrations. Comport yourselves so that our conquerors will respect us.

"Beyond that I have no advice to give. The terms of surrender will reach me in due course and will be immediately communicated to you. Until then may God bless you all and stay you in this hour of trial."

There was a long pause, and the radio said:

"Ladies and gentlemen, the President of the United States."

"My fellow Americans. Our armed forces have met with . . . "

Justin looked around him incredulously and saw that most of them were silently crying.

CHAPTER TWO

Along about one o'clock people began to drift dazedly from the store—to their homes in Norton to talk in stunned whispers on the board sidewalk fronting the grocery. Old man Croley turned the radio off when a girl's voice said between replays of the surrender statement that there would be a new announcement broadcast at 9:00 P.M. for which electric-current restrictions would be temporarily relaxed.

"That'll be the surrender terms," Gus Feinblatt said to Justin.

"I guess so. Gus—what do you think?"

There were four thousand years of dark history in Feinblatt's eyes. "I think the worst is yet to come, Billy."

"You'll get your kids back."

"At such a price. I don't know whether it's worth it . . . Well, life goes on. Mr. Croley?"

The storekeeper looked up. He didn't say "Yes?" or "What can I do for you?" He never did; he looked and he waited and he never called anybody by name. He wasn't an old-timer as old-timers went in Norton; he had come ten years ago from a grocery in Minnesota, and had used those ten years well. Justin knew he sold hardware, fencing, coal, fuel oil, fertilizer, feed and seed—in short, everything a farmer needed to earn his living —as well as groceries. Justin suspected that he also ran a small private bank which issued loans at illegal rates of interest. He did know that there were farmers who turned pale when Croley looked speculatively at them, and farm wives who cursed him behind his back. He was sixty-five, childless, and married to an ailing, thin woman who spent most of her time in the apartment above the store.

"Mr. Croley," Gus said, "I might as well get my feed. My wagon's outside the storeroom."

Croley put out his hand and waited. Gus laid twenty-seven dollars in it, and still the hand was out, waiting. "Coupons?" Gus asked wryly.

"You heard him," Croley said. (After a moment you figured out that "him" was the President, who had said that civilians were to continue as before, maintaining order.) Gus tore ration coupons out of his "F" book and laid them on the money. The hand was

withdrawn and Croley stumped outside to un-
lock the storeroom door and stand by,
watching, as Feinblatt and Justin loaded
sacks of feed onto the stake wagon. When the
last one went *bump* on the bed, he relocked
the door, turned, and went back into his
grocery.

"Gus," Justin said, "would you mind
waiting a minute? I want to see if Croley
happens to have a pump rod for me—and then
I'd like to bum a ride home from you."

"Glad to have your company," Feinblatt
said, politely abstracted.

Croley listened to Justin in silence, reached
under his counter, and banged a pump rod
down in front of his customer. He snapped:
"Twelve-fifty without hardware coupon.
Three-fifty with."

The old skunk knew, of course, that Justin
had used up his quarterly allotment of
hardware coupons to fix his milker. Justin
paid, red-faced with anger, and went out to
climb alongside Feinblatt on the wagon. Gus
clucked at the horses and they moved off.

Rumble-rumble over the Lehigh tracks and
up Straw Hill Road, with Tony and Phony
pulling hard on the stiff grade, the wagon
wheels crashing into three years of unfixed
chuckholes. Halfway up Feinblatt called
"Whoa" and fixed the brake. "Rest 'em a
little," he said to Justin. "All they get's hay, of
course. Feed has to go to the cows. How's
your herd?"

"All right, I guess," Justin said. "I wonder if
I can let 'em go now. You want to buy them? I

guess I don't get drafted for a road gang now if I stop farming."

"Think again," Feinblatt said. "My guess is you better stick to exactly what you've been doing. Things are going to keep on this way for a while—maybe quite a while. You know about the postal service in the Civil War?"

Feinblatt was the local Civil War fanatic; every community seemed to have one. They spent vacations touring the battlefields ecstatically, comparing the ground with the maps. They had particular heroes among the generals and they loved to guess at what would have happened if this successful raid had failed, if that disastrous skirmish had been a triumph.

"Lincoln called for volunteers," Gus Feinblatt said impressively. "Carolina fired on Fort Sumter. The war was on. And yet for *months* there was no interruption of the U.S. mail between the two countries. Inertia, you call it. So maybe even if there isn't any war left to fight now, maybe even if the Reds kick the President and Congress out of Underground, D.C., there will still be people on the state and local level to enforce drafting you for labor if you quit farming." He released the brake and clucked to the horses. The bay geldings strained up the hill again.

"I guess you're right," Justin said reluctantly. "Things won't be squared away for a long while. I guess after things get settled, they replace government people with Reds, if they can find enough." He laughed unpleasantly. "Wait and see what happens to that snake Croley then! If ever there was any-body who qualified in the Commie book as a dirty capitalist exploiter it's our buddy down in Norton."

Feinblatt shrugged. "He made his bed. When I think my boys were fighting for *him*—!" He spat over the side of the wagon, his face flushed.

"What do you hear from them?" Justin hastily asked. He had stopped one in Korea, but was guiltily aware that there was a keener agony of war that he had never known—the father's agony.

"Card from Daniel last week. Infantry re-placement training center in Montana. He was just finishing his basic. We worked out a kind of code, so I know he was hoping they wouldn't ship him South as a rifleman, but he thought they might. He was bucking for 75-millimeter recoilless gunner. It would have kept him on ice for another two weeks. From David not a word since he joined the 270th at El Paso. I don't know, Billy. I just don't know. It's over, sure, they'll come back maybe, but I don't know . . . . "

There was little more talk from then on. "Here's where I get off," Justin said at last. "My best to Leah." He swung down at his mailbox and limped down the steep hill to his house. May be able to get some decent shoes after things settle down, he thought bitterly. That'll be something.

It still did not seem real.

Obviously things were badly disorganized somewhere. The house lights kept going on and off; the phone rang his number now and then, but when he answered there was only the open-circuit hum of a broken line. He couldn't call anybody himself. He had a useless electric clock on the mantel which told him that the electric service was going badly off the beam. He timed the second hand with his watch and discovered that the alternating current delivered to his house was wobbling between 30 and 120 cycles per second instead of flowing at an even 60 per. A bomb at Niagara? Fighting for a power substation somewhere? Engineers quitting their posts in despair?

But the Eastern Milkshed Administration truck had picked up his milk cans while he was gone. He herded his cows into the barn, belatedly washed the milker and pails, and relieved their full udders once more. God alone knew whether the milk would ever reach (cholera-ridden?) New York City, but the mail would go through, the EMA truck driver would report him if there were no cans to pick up, and the administrative machinery of a nation which was no longer alive would grind him through the gears into a road-mending crew whether it mattered a damn or not.

Once during the afternoon somebody goofed at the local radio station, which was rebroadcasting the message of capitulation. A woman's voice screamed hysterically: "Rally, Americans! Fight the godless Reds! Fight them in the streets, from behind bushes, house to house—" And then, whoever she was, somebody dragged her away from the mike and said wearily: "We regret the interruption of our service due to circumstances beyond our control." Then, again: "Ladies and gentlemen, the President of the United States."

"My fellow Americans. Our armed forces have met with a—"

The current went off again, this time for an hour.

There was a calm, slow knock on the door. Through the kitchen window Justin recognized Mister, sometimes The Reverend Mister Sparhawk. Sparhawk happened to be the last man on Earth whom he wanted to see at the moment. He also happened to be a man practically impossible to insult, completely impervious to hints, maddeningly certain of his righteousness.

Justin sighed and opened the door. "Come on in," he told the lean old man. "Just, for God's sake, don't talk. Find something to eat and go away." He opened his breadbox and retreated into the living room hoping he wouldn't be pursued. Sparhawk was a ref, an Englishman. Justin was sick of refs, and so was everybody. The refs from the Baltic, the Balkans, Germany, France, England, Latin America—he vaguely felt that they ought to have stayed in their countries and been exterminated instead of bothering Americans. English refs were the least obnoxious, they didn't *jabber*, but Sparhawk—

The lean old man came into the living room eating bread and cheese. "Buck up, m' boy," Sparhawk said cheerily. "All this is only a Trial, you know. You should regard it as a magnificent opportunity. Here's your chance to play the man, acquire merit, and get a leg up on your next incarnation."

"Oh, shut up," Justin said.

"Natural reaction, very. I don't blame you a bit, m'boy. But sober reflection on the great events of this day will show you their spiritual meaning. How else would you haughty Americans get the chance to humble yourselves and practice asceticism if there were no Red occupation?"

Justin studied Sparhawk's neatly pressed garb, a collection of donated items in good repair. He snapped: "If you're so damned ascetic, why don't you go around in a jock-strap like your beloved yogis?"

Sparhawk stiffened ever so slightly. "My dear young man," he said, "Anybody who wore only a loincloth in your atrocious climate might or might not be a saint, but he'd certainly be a bloody fool. I see you're in no mood for serious discussion, sir. I'll bid you good day."

"Good riddance," Justin muttered, but only after Sparhawk had shouldered his rucksack again and was going down the kitchen steps.

At about seven in the evening Justin decided to visit his friends the Bradens a mile and a half up the battered road. He hadn't seen much of them during the winter; his meager gas allotment had been cut to zero in the general reduction of last November. He had missed them personally, missed their off-beat chatter and Amy's generously shared home brew. The only other liquor in the area was a vicious grape brandy illegally distilled by old Mr. Konreid on Ash Hill Road. It put you under fast. The next morning you wished you would die.

Lew Braden had a weird profession. He was a maker of fine hand-laid papers for book-binders and etchers. Before the war it was his custom to tour the country each summer in a battered Ford offering picayune prices to farm wives for their soft old linen tablecloths and napkins, washed thousands of times, worn to rags, and stored thriftily in an attic trunk. He would finish his tour with bales of the inimitable material and spend the winter turning it, with the aid of simple tools, dexterity, and a great deal of know-how, into inimitable special-purpose papers. The Braden watermark was internationally famous—to about five hundred bookbinders and etchers—and he cleared perhaps three thousand dollars in an average year. It was, he often said nostalgically, a very easy buck. Under the Farm-or-Fight Law he and Amy had elected to start a piggery and truck farm for the reason that it required less effort than dairying or field crops. They turned out to be right. They had sailed through three years of war without much trouble, with time to read, paint, play violin-piano duets, and drink.

Justin, chained to the twice-daily milking and the niggling hygiene of the milkhouse, envied their good sense.

Good sense, he thought, picking his way around the chuckholes in the moonlit road—maybe they can explain to me what the devil has happened and what happens next.

The countryside was winking on and off in the dusk like a Christmas tree. The Horbath farm up the hill, the Parry farm to the south with its big yard light, his own house behind him alternately flared with lights in every window and then went out. He hoped the current would steady down by nine—time for "the further announcement."

Lew Braden prudently called as he entered their dark yard: "Who's there? I've got a shotgun!"

"It's Justin," he called back.

The yard light went on and stayed on. Braden studied him with a mild perplexity. "Darned if you aren't," he said. "Come in, Billy. We were hoping somebody'd drop by. What's going on with the lights and the phone?"

"You haven't heard?"

"Obviously not. Come in and tell us about it, whatever it is. Nobody's been by and the radio won't go since Amy fixed it."

The radio was indeed roaring unintelligibly on an end table.

"It's over," Justin said. "That's what it's all about. Fraley surrendered at El Paso. The President capitulated through the embassies in Switzerland. They've been broadcasting it since noon. Let me see that damned radio. It sounds as if you just haven't got it on a station."

He pulled the chassis out of the plastic case and saw the trouble. The cord from the tuning-knob pulley to the variable condenser was slack instead of taut; the radio worked but you couldn't tune it from the knob. He picked up a stub of pencil and shoved the condenser over to one of the CONELRAD stations.

" . . . in-Chief of the Armed Forces of the United States I now order all officers and enlisted men to cease fire. Maintain discipline, hold your ranks . . . "

They listened to it twice through and then turned it down. Between each of the replays now the woman's voice announced that a further statement would be made at nine.

Lew and Amy were looking at each other. The expression on their faces was unreadable. At last Lew turned to Justin and said softly: "Don't worry about a thing, Billy. You're going to have to make a big readjustment in your thinking, but so will almost everybody. You'll find out you've been fed a pack of lies. You'll fight the truth at first, but finally we'll prove to you—"

"We? Who's *we?"* Justin demanded.

"Shut up, Lew," Amy said briefly.

He turned his kindly, round bespectacled face to her. "No, Amy. You, too, are having difficulty in readjusting. Conditions have changed now; we're suddenly no longer conspirators but the voice and leadership of

America. A new America."

Guilelessly he turned again to Justin. 'We're Communists, Billy. Have been for twenty years. This is the grandest day of my life."

Justin felt an impulse to back away. "You're kidding. Or crazy!"

"Neither one, Billy. You see, this is the first of the readjustments you will have to make. You think a Communist must necessarily be a fiend, a savage, a foreigner. You couldn't conceive of a Communist being a soft-spoken, reasonable, mannerly person. But Amy and I are, aren't we? And we're Communists. When I was on those linen-buying trips, I was doubling as a courier. I was in the Party category you call 'floaters' then. Since the war I've been what you call a 'sleeper.' No conspiratorial activity, no connection with the activist branch. I have merely been under orders to hold myself in readiness for this day. I know who lives hereabouts, I know their sentiments. I am, I think, almost everybody's friend. My job will be to educate the people of this area.

"You see? Your education is beginning already. There will be no brutal, foreign tyrants around here. There will be Amy and me— friends and neighbors—just the way we always were, explaining to you the new America.

"And what an America it will be! Freed from the shackles of capitalist exploitation and racial hatred! Purged of the warmongers who imposed a crushing armament burden on the workers and finally goaded the U.S.S.R.

and the C.P.R. into attacking! An America freed from bondage to ancient superstition!"

There were tears of joy in his eyes.

Justin asked slowly: "Have you spied? Have you been traitors?"

Lew said with dignity:

"You're thinking of cloak-and-dagger stuff, Billy. Assassination. Break open the locked drawer and steal the great atomic secret for godless Russia. Well, there was a little melodrama, but I never liked it. I've risked my life more than once and I was glad to. Amy and I were couriers; DoD papers passed through our hands. It was only by a fluke that the FBI didn't stumble onto us. If they had, I suppose we would have fried. Gladly. For America, Billy. Because I did not spy against the people. I did not commit treason against the people."

Justin said: "Good night, Lew. Good night, Amy. I don't know what to think . . . ."

Lew said confidently to his back: "You'll readjust. It'll be all right. Don't worry."

He walked home and found that the current was on again, apparently for good. He climbed to the attic and brought down a half-full gallon of old Mr. Konreid's popskull. He filled a tumbler and sipped at it until nine, when the radio said:

"Ladies and gentlemen, the Secretary of State."

"Fellow citizens, I have been ordered to communicate to you the Articles of Surrender which were signed in Washington, D.C., today by the President on behalf of the United States, by Marshal Ilya Novikov on behalf of the Union of Soviet Socialist Republics, and by Marshal Feng Chu-tsai on behalf of the Chinese People's Republic.

"One. The United States surrenders without conditions to the Soviet Union and the C.P.R. Acts of violence against troops of the Soviet Union and the C.P.R. on or after April 17 are recognized by the high contracting parties as criminal banditry and terrorism, subject to summary and condign punishment.

"Two. The high contracting parties recognize and admit the criminal guilt of the United States in provoking the late war and recognize and admit the principle that the United States is liable to the Soviet Union and the C.P.R. for indemnities in *valuta* and kind.

"Three. The high contracting parties recognize and admit the *personal* criminal war guilt of certain civilians and soldiers of the United States and recognize and admit that these persons are subject to condign punishment."

The Secretary's voice shook. "I have been further asked to announce that the central functions of the United States Federal Government were assumed today by Soviet Military Government Unit 101, which today arrived by air in Washington, D.C., under the escort of two Russian and two Chinese airborne divisions.

"I have been further asked to announce that under Article Three of the Articles of

Surrender I read you the President and Vice-
President of the United States were shot to
death at eight o'clock, P.M., by a mixed
Russian and Chinese firing squad."

That was all.

Justin's hand was trembling so the raw
brandy slopped over the tumbler's edge.

CHAPTER THREE

April 23, seventh day of the defeat . . .

Justin leaned on his mailbox waiting for Betsy Cardew, his morning chores behind him, and reflected that things had gone with amazing smoothness. Nor was there any particular reason why they shouldn't. Soviet Military Government Unit 101 had certainly planned and practiced for twenty years. The Baltic states, the Balkans, Poland, Czechoslovakia, East Germany, West Germany, France, Italy, Spain, and England—they had been priceless rehearsals for the main event.

And what a main event! Half the world's steel, coal and oil. All the world's free helium gas. Midwest grain, northwest timber, and the magnificent road net to haul them to magnifi-

cent ports. Industrial New England, shabby
streets and dingy factories, but in the dingy
factories the world's finest precision tools.
Detroit! South Bend! Prizes that made all the
loot of all the conquerors of history flashy
junk. SMGU 101 would not let the plunder slip
through its fingers. It was moving fast,
moving smoothly.

For the greatest part of the loot, the part
without which the materials would be worthless, consisted of 230 million Americans. They
knew how to extract that steel, coal and gas,
harvest the grain, log the forests, drive the
trucks, load the freighters, run the lathes and
punch presses.

Betsy Cardew had yesterday delivered to
him—and to everybody on her route—SMGU
Announcement Number One, so Gus Feinblatt
was right. They turned over a carload of
SMGU announcements to the Postmaster,
D.C., with the note "one to each address," and
it was automatic from there. The carload was
broken down by regions, states, counties,
towns, rural routes, and three days later
everybody had one in his hand.

They hadn't been using radio. When current
was on, and it was on more and more frequently as the days went by, all you heard
were light-classical music, station breaks, and
the time.

The SMGU announcement didn't come to
much. It was simply a slanted recap of the
military situation, larded with praise of
General Fraley and his troops, expressing
gentle regret that so many fine young men

and women had been lost to both sides. As an afterthought it stated: "The nationalization of all fissionable material is hereby proclaimed, and all Americans are notified that they must turn in any private stores of uranium, thorium, or plutonium, either elemental or combined, to the nearest representative of the U.S.S.R. or C.P.R. at once."

Justin decided the first announcement must have been a test shot to find out how well the distribution would work. Its message certainly was pointless.

Betsy Cardew pulled up in the battered car. Lew and Amy Braden were in the back. She said: "No mail today, Billy. Do you want a ride in? Mr. and Mrs. Braden here were first, but there's room."

"Thanks," he said, and got in. He couldn't think of one word to say to his former friends, but they had no such trouble.

"I've been called to Chiunga Center," Lew said importantly. Chiunga Center was *the* town thereabouts: twenty thousand people in a bend of the Susquehanna, served by the Lehigh and the Lackawanna. "Advance units have reached the town."

"Yesterday," Betsy said. "A regiment, I guess, in trucks. Very G.I., very Russian, very much on their good behavior. They're barracked in the junior high. They set up a mess tent on the campus and strung barbed wire. Nine-o'clock curfew in town and patrols with tommy guns. So far everything's quiet. A couple of kids threw rocks." She laughed abruptly. "I saw it. I thought the sergeant was going to cut them in half with his tommy gun but he didn't. He took down their pants and *spanked* them."

"Smart cooky," Lew said gravely from the back of the car. "He played it exactly right."

"So," said Betsy, "there I am in the post-office sorting room busy sorting and in march six of them, polite as you please, and say through the window, 'Ve vish to see the post-mahster,' and old Flanahan comes tottering out ready to die like a man. So they hand him six letters. 'Pliss to expedite delivery of these, Mr. Postmahster,' they say, and *salute* him and go away. And one of the letters is for Mr. and Mrs. Braden here and they won't tell me what it's all about, but they don't look like a couple going to their doom and I'm too well-trained a postal employee to pry."

Her flow of chatter was almost hysterical and Justin thought he knew why. It was the hysteria of relief, the discovery that the Awful Thing, the thing you dreaded above all else, has happened and isn't too bad after all. Chiunga Center was occupied, taken, conquered, seized—and life went on after all, and you felt a little foolish over your earlier terror. The Russians were just G.I.s, and weren't you a fool to think they had horns?

"You see?" Lew Braden said to nobody in particular.

"What *I* think," Betsy chattered, "is that they're just as dumb as any army men anywhere. You know what the first poster they stuck up said? Turn in your uranium and plutonium at once. The dopes! The *second* notice covered pistols, rifles, shotguns, and bayonets. That touch of idiocy is almost cute. Bayonets!''

They had reached State Highway 19 and stopped; Norton lay dead ahead and Chiunga Center was fourteen miles to the right on the highway. A convoy of trucks marked with the red star was rolling westward at maybe thirty-five. They were clean, well-maintained trucks and they were full of Russian soldiers in Class A uniforms. They caught a snatch of mournful harmony and the rhythmic nasal drone of a concertina.

"My Lord!" Betsy said. "They really do sing all the time. And in minor fifths. I thought they were putting it on at the mess tent, impressing the Amerikanskis with their culture and soul, but there isn't any audience here."

The last of the convoy, a couple of slum-guns, field kitchens like any army's field kitchens complete to the fat personnel, rolled past and Justin realized that they were waiting for him to get out and proceed on foot to Norton.

"Take it easy," he said to the Bradens, and watched the car swing right and pick up high-way speed. The Bradens were about to enter into their own peculiar version of the kingdom of heaven. He himself needed another pump rod. The one Croley sold him turned out to be a painted white metal casting instead of rolled steel. It had, of course snapped the first time he used it.

Perce, Croley's literally half-witted

assistant, waved gaily at him as he approached the store. Perce bubbled over: "Gee, you should of seen 'im, mister, I bet he was a general or maybe a major. Boy, he came right into the store and he looked just like anybody else on'y he was a *Red!* Right into the store. Boy!"

Perce couldn't get over the wonder of it, and Justin, examining himself, was not sure that he could either. When would this thing seem *real?* Maybe it seemed real in the big cities, but his worm's-eye view frustrated his curiosity and sense of drama. It was like sitting behind a post in a theater, only the play was *The Decline and Fall of the United States of America.* A Russian—a general or maybe a major—appeared and then disappeared. The local underground Reds were summoned to service—where and what? The convoy passed you on the road, to duty where?

Croley was tacking up a notice, a big one, that covered his bulletin board, buried the ration-book notices, the draft-call notices, the buy-bonds poster. It said:

SOVIET MILITARY

GOVERNMENT

Unit 449
Chiunga County, New York State

Residents are advised that effective at once,

the following temporary measures will be observed:

1. A curfew is established from Nine O'Clock P.M. to Five O'Clock A.M. All residents must be in their homes between these hours.

2. Fissionable material must be turned in to this command at once since uranium, thorium, and plutonium have been declared nationalized and unlawful for any private person to hold.

3. All privately held pistols, rifles, shotguns, and bayonets must be turned in to this command or representative. For the township of _____ this command's representative is _____. The weapons should be tagged with the owner's name and address and will later be returned.

4. Violators of these measures will be subject to military trial and if found guilty liable to sixty days in jail.

> *S.P. Platov*
> *Colonel, Commanding*

Justin shook his head slowly. Sixty days! Was *this* the Red barbarian they had all been dreading? He seemed to hear Lew Braden saying again: "Smart cooky . . . exactly right."

Croley had gone behind his counter for something, a price-marking crayon. He was filling in the blanks in Number 3. "For the township of NORTON this command's representative is FLOYD C. CROLEY. The weapons should—"

Croley stepped back, looked for a moment at the black, neat printing, stuck the crayon behind his ear, and turned to Justin, waiting and blank-faced.

Justin asked: "Since when have you represented the Red Army?"

Croley said: "He wanted a central place. Somebody steady." And that was supposed to dispose of that. O.K., you skunk, Justin thought. Wait until my two traitorous friends blow the whistle on *you*. When the Bradens finish telling the Reds all about Floyd C. Croley, Floyd C. Croley will be very small potatoes around these parts, or possibly Siberia. And aloud: "You sold me a dog, Mr. Croley. Look at this crumby thing."

He slapped down the two broken halves of the cheap cast pump rod. Croley picked them up, turned them over in his hands, and put them down again. "Never guaranteed it," he said.

"For twelve-fifty it shouldn't break on the first stroke, Mr. Croley. I need a pump rod and I insist on a replacement."

Croley picked the pieces up again and examined them minutely. He said at last: "Allow you ten dollars on a fifteen-dollar rod. Steel. No coupons."

And that, Justin realized, was as good a deal as he'd ever get from the old snake. Too disgusted to talk, he slapped down a ten-dollar bill. Croley took it, produced another rod, and a queer-looking five-dollar bill in change. The portrait was of a hot-eyed young man identified by the little ribbon as John Reed. Instead of "The United States of America," it said: "The North American People's Democratic Republic."

Justin's voice broke as he yelled: "What are you trying to put over, Croley? Give me a real bill, damn you!"

Croley shrugged patiently. A take-it-or-leave-it shrug. He condescended to explain: "He bought gas. It's good enough for him, it's good enough for me. Or you." And turned away to fiddle with the rack in which he kept the credit books of his customers.

Speechless, Justin rammed the phony bill into his pocket, picked up the rod, and walked away. As he opened the door, the old man's voice came sharply: "Justin."

He turned. Croley said: "Watch your mouth, Justin." He jerked his thumb at the announcement. (" . . .representative is FLOYD C. CROLEY. The weapons . . . ") He went back to his credit books as Justin stared incredulously, torn between laughter and disgust.

He walked out and across the Lehigh tracks. Nobody seemed to be in town; he was in for a four-mile walk, mostly uphill, to his place. The cows would be milked late—he quickened his pace.

At the highway a couple of Russian soldiers beside a parked jeep were just finishing erecting a roadside sign—blue letters on white, steel backing, steel post, fired enamel front. They hadn't rushed *that* out in six days. The sign had been waiting in a Red Army warehouse for this day, waiting perhaps twenty years. It said: "CHECK POINT 200 YARDS AHEAD. ALL CIVILIAN VEHICLES STOP FOR INSPECTION." That would be the old truck-weighing station, reactivated as a road block.

The Russians were a corporal and a private, both of the tall, blond, Baltic type. They had a slung tommy gun apiece. He said: "Hi, boys."

The private grinned, the corporal scowled and said: *"Nye ponimayoo.* Not per-mitten."

He wanted to say something witty and cutting, something about sourpusses, or the decadent plutocrat contaminating the pure proletarian, or how the corporal might make sergeant if his English were better. He looked at the tommy guns instead, shrugged, and walked on. Yes, he was scared. With the vivid imagination of an artist he could see the slugs tearing him. So the rage against Croley festered still, and the taste of defeat was still sour in his mouth. And he still had four uphill miles to walk to milk those loathesome cows of his.

By nine that night he was thinking of starting to work on Mr. Konreid's brandy. The current was on and, according to his electric clock, steady. He had lost the radio habit during the silent years. There was now apparently only one station on the air and it offered gems from *Mademoiselle Modiste.* He didn't want them. He leafed over a few of his art books and found them dull. Somewhere in the attic a six-by-eight printing press and a font of type were stashed, but he didn't feel like digging them out to play with. That had been one of the plans for his retirement. Old Mr. Justin would amuse himself by pottering with the press, turning out minuscule private editions of the shorter classics on Braden's beautiful hand-laid paper. Maybe old Mr. Justin would clear expenses, maybe not—

But now he was too sick at heart to think of the shorter classics and Braden was much too busy securing his appointment as Commissar of Norton Township or something to contribute the beautiful paper.

The phone rang two longs, his call. It was a girl's voice that he didn't recognize at first.

"It's Betsy," she said with whispered urgency. "No names. Your two friends—remember this morning?"

Yes; yes. The Bradens. Well? "Yes. I remember."

"In the basement of the school. The janitor saw the bodies before they took them away. They were shot. You knew them. I—I thought I ought to tell you. They must have been very brave. I never suspected—"

"Thanks," he said. "Good-by," and hung up.

Betsy thought the Bradens were some kind of heroic anti-Communists.

Then he began to laugh, hysterically. He could reconstruct it perfectly. The Marshal said to the General: "The first thing we've got to do is get rid of the damn Red troublemakers." And so it trickled down to "Pliss to expedite delivery of these, Mr. Postmahster," and so the Bradens got their summons and, unsuspecting, were taken down-cellar and shot because, as Braden knew, those Reds were very smart cookies indeed. They knew, from long experience, that you don't want trained revolutionaries kicking around in a country you've just whipped, revolutionaries who know how to hide and subvert and betray, because all of a sudden *you* are stability and order, and trained revolutionaries are a menace.

No, what you wanted instead of revolutionaries were people like Croley.

Croley!

He couldn't stop laughing. When he thought of thousands of underground American Communists lying tonight in their own blood on thousands of cellar floors, when he thought of Floyd C. Croley, Hero of Soviet Labor, Servant of the North American People's Democratic Republic, he couldn't stop laughing.

CHAPTER FOUR

April 30 . . .

The first of the spring rains had come and gone. They were broadcasting weather forecasts again, which was good. You noticed that forecasts east of the Mississippi were credited to the Red Air Force Meteorological Service. From the Mississippi to the Pacific it was through the courtesy of the Weather Organization of the Chinese People's Republic. Apparently this meant that the two Communist powers had split the continent down the middle. China got more land, which it badly needed, and Russia got more machinery, which *it* badly needed. A very logical solution of an inevitable problem.

The Sunday *Times* had stopped coming, but

Justin hardly missed it. He was a farmer, whether he liked it or not, and spring was his busy season. He had grudged time to attend the auction of the Bradens' estate, but once there he had picked up some badly needed tools and six piglets. Croley, under whose general authority the auction was held, himself bought the house and twelve acres for an absurd eight hundred dollars. Nobody bid against him, but after the place was knocked down to him, half a dozen farmers tried to rent it. They were thinking of their sons and daughters in the service who should be back very soon. Croley grudgingly allowed the Wehrweins to have the place at fifty dollars a month, cash or kind.

Justin was almost happy on the spring morning that was the fourteenth day of defeat. His future looked clear for the moment. The red clover was sprouting bravely in his west pasture; he'd be able to turn his cows out any day now and still have hay in reserve. Electric service was steady; he'd be able to run a single-strand electric fence instead of having to break his back repairing and tightening the wartime four-strand nonelectric fences. The piglets looked promising; he anticipated an orgy of spareribs in the fall and all the ham, bacon, and sausage he could eat through the winter. His two dozen bantams were gorging themselves on the bugs of spring and laying like mad; it meant all the eggs he wanted and plenty left over for the Eastern Milkshed Administration pickup. His vegetable garden was spaded and ready for seeding; his long years of weed chopping seemed to have suddenly paid off. There wasn't a sign of plantain, burdock, or ironweed anywhere on his place.

At ten-thirty the EMA truck ground to a stop at his roadside platform and even McGinty, the driver, was cheery with spring. He loaded the cans and handed Justin his monthly envelope—and stood by, grinning, waiting for Justin to open it. Justin understood the gag when a few of the new phony bills fluttered from the statement. He counted up ninety-three dollars in Bill Haywood ones, John Reed fives, and Lincoln Steffens tens. He didn't give McGinty the satisfaction of seeing him blow his top. As a matter of fact, he wasn't particularly upset. If everybody agreed that this stuff was money, then it *was* money. He murmured: "Paying in cash now? I guess that means I sign a receipt."

McGinty, bitterly disappointed, produced a receipt book and a stub of pencil. "You should of heard old lady Wehrwein," he said reminiscently. Justin checked the statement (Apr 1-Apr 15 a/c Justin WH, Norton Twp Chiµnga Cy, 31 cwt at $3.00, $93.00) and signed. McGinty's truck rumbled on.

It was a miserably small two-week net for eight good Holsteins, but they were near the end of their lactation period; soon he'd have to arrange for freshening them again.

He was planting onion sets and radish seed in his vegetable garden when Rawson came down the road—the legless veteran whom he had met on the day of defeat. Rawson turned up at the estate sale and he found out that he had indeed got work at the Shiptons' farm, but for how long was anybody's guess, with the Shiptons' three boys and two girls due for demobilization.

Rawson seemed to be in a hell of a hurry to get to him. Justin straightened up and met him at the road. "What's up?"

"Plenty, Billy. Couple of Red Army boys over at the Shiptons'. One's a farm expert, the other's an interpreter. They're going over the place with a fine-tooth comb. Boils down to this: the Shiptons have to turn out 25 per cent more milk, 10 per cent more grain, and God knows what else. The old lady told me to pass the word around. Fake your books, hide one of your cows—whatever you can think of. Push me off, will you? I've got some more ground to cover."

"Thanks," Justin said thoughtfully, and pushed. The little cart went spinning down the road, Rawson, pumping away. He called it "my muscle-mobile."

Justin mechanically went back to his onion sets and radish seed, but the savor had gone out of the spring morning. He couldn't think of one right, definite thing to do. He didn't come from twenty generations of farmers consummately skilled at looking poor when they were rich. He didn't know the thousand dodges farmers everywhere always used, almost instinctively, to cheat the tax man of his due for the tsar, the commissar, the emperor, the shereef, the zamindar, La

Republique, the American Way of Life. Billy Justin, like a fool, kept books—and only one set of them. He was a sitting duck.

The jeep with the red star arrived in mid-afternoon while he was mending fence in the pasture with a sledge, block and tackle, nippers and pliers. In spite of his heavy gloves he had got a few rips from the rusted, snarled old wire. He was feeling savage. He heard them honk for him, deliberately finished driving a cedar post, and then slowly strolled toward the road.

Two privates were in the front seat, chauffeur and armed guard, two officers in the back, a captain and a lieutenant. Both young, both sweating in too-heavy wool dress uniforms with choker collars, both festooned with incomprehensible ribbons and decorations.

The lieutenant said, looking up from a typewritten list, "You're Mr. William H. Justin, aren't you?"

Justin gulped. To hear the flat, midwest American speech coming from this fellow in this uniform was a jolt. It made the whole thing seem like a fancy-dress party. "Yes," he said. And then, inevitably, "You speak English very well."

"Thanks, Mr. Justin. I worked hard at it. I'm Lieutenant Zoloty of the 449th Military Government Unit. Translator. And this is Captain Kirilov of the same command. He's the head of our agronomy group."

Kirilov, bored, jerked a nod at Justin.

"We'd like to look over your layout as part

of a survey we're running. I see you're listed as primarily a dairy farmer, so let's start with your cow barn and milkhouse."

"Right this way," Justin said flatly.

Captain Kirilov knew his stuff. He scowled at the unwashed milker, felt the bags of the eight Holsteins, kicked disapprovingly at a rotten board. Through it all he directed a stream of Russian at Zoloty, who nodded and took notes. Once the captain got angry. He was burrowing through the corncrib and found rat droppings. He shook them under Justin's nose and yelled at him. After he disgustedly cast them aside and wiped his hands on a corn shuck, the lieutenant said in a undertone: "He was explaining that rodents are intolerable on a well-run farm, that grain should be raised for the people and not for parasites."

"Uh-huh," Justin said.

When the captain came across the six piglets, he was delighted. Zoloty said: "The captain is pleased that there are six. He says, 'At last I see the famous American principle of mass production. Our peasants at home wastefully indulge in roast-pig feasts instead of letting all the young grow to maturity.'"

Finally the captain snapped something definite and final, left the barn, and headed for the jeep.

Zoloty said: "Captain Kirilov establishes your norm at twenty hundredweight of milk per week. Do you understand what that means?"

"I know what twenty hundredweight of

milk is. I don't know what a norm is."

"It is your quota. If you fall below twenty hundredweight per week consistently, or if your production fails to average out to that, you will be subject to review."

Zoloty started to turn away.

"Lieutenant, what does 'review' mean?"

"Your farming techniques will be studied. If you need a short course to improve your efficiency, you'll be given an opportunity to take it. We're organizing them up at Cornell. Or it may turn out that you're just temperamentally unsuited for farming. In that case we may have to look for a slot where you'll function more efficiently."

"Road gang?" Justin asked quietly.

Zoloty was embarrassed. "Please don't be truculent, Mr. Justin. Why should we put an intelligent person like you on a road gang? Now please come along to the jeep. Military Intelligence drafted us for another survey they're running. It'll only take a moment."

Justin managed to conceal his relief. He could manage twenty hundredweight a week very easily. Just a little more care to the herd's diet, get that rock-salt brick he'd been letting slide, promise the Shiptons a hog in the fall for some of their hoarded cottonseed cake.It would be a breeze, and Rawson had been unduly alarmed. But farmers had this habit of screaming bloody murder at the least little thing. He hated to admit it, but the red-star boys were being more than fair about it. He had drifted into sloppy farming.

At the jeep again Zoloty got out some

papers and said: "Now, Mr. Justin, this is official. First, do you have any uranium, thorium, or other fissionable material in your possession?"

Astounded, Justin said: "Of course not!"

"A simple 'No' is sufficient. Sign here, please." He held out one of the papers, his finger indicating the space. Justin read; it was simply a repeat of the statement that he did not have any fissionable materials in his possession. He signed with the lieutenant's pen.

"Thank you. Do you know of any fissionable material that is held by any private parties? Sign here. Thank you. Would you recognize fissionable material if you saw it?"

"I don't think so, Lieutenant."

"Very well then. Please pay attention. Refined uranium, thorium, and plutonium look like lead, but are heavier. A spherical piece of uranium weighing fifty pounds, for instance, would be no larger than a soft ball. Please sign here—it is a simple statement that I have described the appearance of fissionable materials to you. Thank you. Now, would you recognize the components of an atomic bomb if you saw them?"

"No!"

"Very well then. Please pay attention. An atomic bomb is simply a fifty-pound mass of plutonium or uranium-235. Before exploding it consists of two or more pieces. These pieces are slammed together fast and the bomb then explodes. The slamming can be done by placing two pieces at opposite ends of a gun barrel and then blowing them together so they meet in the middle. Or it can be done by placing several chunks of plutonium on the inside of a sphere and then exploding what are called 'shaped charges' so the chunks are driven together into one mass and the atomic bomb proper explodes. Do you understand? Then sign here.

"Now, our Military Intelligence people would like you to swear or affirm that you will immediately report any evidence of fissionable material or atomic-bomb parts in private hands which you may encounter. Do you so swear?"

"I do," Justin said automatically. Zoloty had for a moment grinned wryly—and there had been a sardonic inflection on "Military *Intelligence.*" Hell, no doubt about it—all armies were pretty much alike. Here these two serious people were going about the serious business of stabilizing the country's food supply and some brass hat got a bright idea; saddle them with another job, even if it's a crackpot search for A-bombs in Chiunga County.

He signed. Zoloty handed over a poster, a hastily printed job with hastily drawn line cuts. "Please put this up somewhere in your house, Mr. Justin, and that will be that. Good afternoon."

He spoke to the captain in Russian, the captain spoke to the chauffeur, and away they drove.

Justin studied the poster; it conveyed the same information Zoloty had given him. Atomic bombs! He snorted and went back to his fence mending.

Yes, it seemed the Reds were determined to be firm but fair. Betsy told him there had been a near rape in Chiunga Center one night last week. By the next morning the attacker had been tried, found guilty, and shot against the handball court of the junior high school—a beetle-browed corporal from some eastern province of the U.S.S.R. It hadn't healed the girl, but at least it showed that the Reds were being mighty touchy about their honor.

He chuckled suddenly. Without recording the fact he had noticed that all four of the soldiers in the jeep had wrist watches, good, big chronometer jobs, identical government issue. So the Russians were still sore about their reputation as snatchers of watches, and had taken the one measure that would keep their troops from living up to it: *giving* them all the watches they could use.

Betsy said she and most of the people in the Center were pleasantly surprised. She, in fact, wished that her father hadn't run away. Nobody had even been around asking about him, National Committeeman though he was, yet he was hiding out now in some Canadian muskeg living on canned soup and possibly moose meat—though Betsy doubted that old T.C. was capable of bringing down a moose. She hoped he would drift back when the word got to him that the red-star boys' ferocity had been greatly exaggerated.

She saw Colonel Platov every now and then from a distance; he was the big brass of SMGU 449. He looked like a middle-aged career soldier, no more and no less. He seemed to be a bug on spit and polish. People observed him bawling out sentries over buttons and shoelaces and suchlike. There were always plenty of K.P.s in the mess tent on the high school campus.

What else was new? Well, there was a twenty-four-hour guard on each of the town's two liquor shops to keep soldiers from looting or trying to purchase. There seemed to be movies every evening in the school auditorium. There was a ferocious physical-fitness program going on; SMGU 449 started the day with fifty knee bends, fifty straddle hops, and fifty pushups, from Platov on down, rain or shine, on the athletic field. They also played soccer when off duty and they sang interminably. Wherever there were more than two Russians gathered with nothing to do, out came a concertina or a uke-sized balalaika and they were off.

A big, fat cook shopped in town for the officers' mess, which must be located in the school cafeteria. The enlisted men lived on tea, breakfast slop called *kasha*, black bread, jam, and various powerful soups involving beef, cabbage, potatoes, and beets. The ingredients came in red-star trucks from the South.

Rumors? Well, she had a few and she was passing them on just for entertainment. The Russians would shortly be joined by their wives. They would close all the churches in Chiunga Center. They would not close any of the churches but instead would forcibly baptize everybody as Greek Orthodox. Demobilization of the United States Army would be completed by next week. Demobilization of the United States Army would be begun next month. The United States Army had disintegrated and the boys and girls were finding their way home on foot. The United States Army Atomic Service had made off with two tons of plutonium from Los Alamos before the surrender—

As that one ran through his mind, Justin suddenly straightened up from the tangled wire.

Two tons of plutonium was enough for eighty atomic bombs. It seemed that any sufficiently reckless machinist could put the bombs together if he had the plutonium.

Two tons of plutonium adrift somewhere in the United States, scattered but in the hands of men who knew what they were doing, might explain quite a few things that had recently puzzled him.

And the thought gave him a stab of painful hope. It let him feel at last the full anguish of the defeat, the reality of it. He burned with shame suddenly for his lick-spittle acceptance of firm-but-fair Lieutenant Zoloty and his gratitude, his disgusting gratitude that they had raised his norm no higher, his pleasure at Captain Kirilov's bored compliment about the pigs.

Suddenly the defeat was real and agonizing. Two tons of plutonium had made it so.

CHAPTER FIVE

"Good drying weather," the radio had been saying for days. Justin, breaking clods and weeding in his cornfield, reflected that once you would have called it the beginning of a serious drought. The passage of two months, however, had made pessimism unfashionable —almost dangerous. Not that he was afraid. Nobody had anything on Billy Justin; he met his quota and he had been left alone . . .

Until now. A jeep was tooting impatiently for him in front of his house. More foolishness, he supposed, with Kirilov and his interpreter. At least it would be a break in the weeding.

There was only one Russian there, however; some kind of sergeant. He said: "Fermer Yoostin?"

"I guess so," Justin said.

The sergeant handed him a sheet of ugly two-column printing on flimsy paper; Russian on the left, English on the right. *Readjustment of Agricultural Norm—W. Justin.* Good! Now, how much were they going to cut from— He hauled up short at the words filled in, "increase 1 cwt per 2 wks."

He said angrily to the sergeant: "In this weather? Kirilov's—mistaken. It can't be done. I'm hauling water for the cows now. And we haven't got DDT. Flies cut down the production. I haven't got a seed-cake quota; my herd's too small. There must be some mistake. Can you take back word to the captain?"

The sergeant, bored, said: *"Ya nye ponimayoo vas."* He held out a clipboard, a ruled form, and a pen. *"Podtverdeet poloocheneyeh."*

Justin said uncertainly: "Speak English? Tell Captain Kirilov?"

Headshake, then, very slowly and patiently, *"Nye—ponimayoo. Nye."* Brandishing the form and pen: *"Poloocheneyeh. Eemyah. Zdyehs."* He pointed to a line; Justin could do nothing but write his name numbly.

The sergeant roared off in a cloud of dust. Justin stood there and spat grit from his mouth. This time no genial interpreter; this time no firm-but-fair agronomist. This time— orders. Quite, unarguable orders.

He noticed the date on the quota form. July 4.

Rawson came visiting in his gocart and

Justin sourly told him his discovery. The legless man shrugged his giant shoulders. "Shiptons got one too," he said. "That's why they sent me over. Didn't want to use the phone. They're thinking about holding kind of a meeting and getting up kind of a petition."

Justin said violently: "The old fools!" And then, slower, "But they *are old*. I guess they just don't get it. Didn't you try to talk them out of it?"

"Me? The hired man? To Sam Shipton that's farmed his farm for sixty years and his father and his gram'pappy before him? I saved my breath. Rather take a little spin in the muscle-mobile than pitch manure any day. I guess I tell them 'No' from you?"

"Of course. But isn't there some way you can try and keep them out of trouble? Explain, for instance, that it isn't like petitioning the highway commissioner to grade a road or put in a new culvert? *Entirely* different?"

"Sam Shipton's an independent farmer, Billy. He's going to stay one if it kills him."

"It may do that, Sarge. Sooner than he thinks."

"Been wondering why you call me 'Sarge.' Matter of fact, I was a bucktail private in the rear rank. Another thing—confidentially. On my own, not the Shiptons. I happen to have a little bit of contraband . . ."

The word covered a lot of ground. Narcotics. Untaxed liquor. Home-grown tobacco. Guns, ammunition—even reloading tools. Any item of Red Army equipment, from a pint of their purple-dye gasoline to a case of their combat rations. Unlicensed scientific equipment and material. It was all posted on the board down at Croley's store in Norton. Not once had Justin heard of anybody being arrested or even chided for violating the rules, though old Mr. Konreid continued to distill and peddle his popskull, and those who smoked up here grew their own tobacco, minimally concealed, with varying success. Guns and ammunition—practically all of it— had been turned in and stood racked and tagged in Croley's storeroom, under Red Army seal. There was a widespread impression that about guns and ammunition the orders were not kidding, that the rest was just the product of some brass hat covering himself for the record. They were farmers up here, but farmers who had been under fire at San Juan Hill, Belleau Wood, Anzio, Huertgen, Iwo, Pyongyang, Recife, Tehuantepec— not one of them but was "army wise."

Why speak of contraband?

"What about it?" Justin asked warily.

Rawson shrugged. "I want to pass it on to a fella I know, but I don't especially want him to come to the Shiptons'. It isn't bulky. I'd just like to drop it off here sometime and he'll come by in a day or less and pick it up."

"Why me?" Justin asked flatly. "Do I look especially like a smuggler?"

"Not especially," Rawson grinned. "Mostly because you live alone. Also because you wouldn't chisel on me. You're a guy who can't be bothered with doing things the crooked way. Old man Konreid lives alone, but he'd rip open the package as soon as I was out of sight, taste it, and then when my friend came, he'd pretend he didn't know what he was talking about."

So it was liquor or drugs or something of the sort. Justin felt pleased that he had got the answer without crude questioning. Not that Rawson would have had anything to do with anything organized which might conceivably bring retribution. The man was a born scrounger, a cutter of not very important corners. He told him: "Drop it off when you want. Any time I can't do a favor for a neighbor I'll close up shop."

"Thanks, Billy," the legless man said. "Push me off, will you?"

At mail time Justin got to wondering if the Fourth of July was a national holiday in the North American People's Democratic Republic, of which he was a citizen. The morning was shot anyway; he strolled up to the mailbox. It was an easier trip than it used to be. As a citizen of the North American People's Democratic Republic he had lost a comfortable layer of fat at the waist.

Betsy Cardew was waiting at the mailbox looking tired.

He said, "Cultural greetings to you, comrade-citizeness-postwoman!"

"Cultural greetings to you, comrade-citizen-milk-farmer. What the heck kept you?"

"July fourth. I dithered around a couple of minutes wondering if you'd be here."

"Oh, the mail must go through," she said vaguely.

"Then where's mine?"

"As a matter of fact, you haven't got anything today. I wanted to talk to you."

"I'm listening."

"You got one of those quota increases?"

"Yes. Fifty pounds more per week. I don't know how I'm going to make it. They can't really expect it from me, can they?"

"They expect it. It went through two weeks ago in Pennsylvania. They've been picking up families who didn't make the norm. Families with the biggest and best farms. They go South in trucks, men, women, and kids. Nobody seems to know where. Then they turn the acreage over to families from marginal farms that couldn't possibly raise a cash crop. Billy, could you make your new norm with a farm hand?"

"You know I can't support a—"

"This farm hand would have his board paid by the SMGU."

"That's different. And what's the catch?"

"He'd be a little nuts. Wait a minute, Billy! Don't let panic make up your mind until I tell you about him.

"You know I'm a nurse's aid three nights a week at Chiunga General. I was in surgery a week ago when they brought this guy in. His name's Gribble. He was in shock and he'd lost plenty of blood. His hands were lacerated and there was a gash along his right forearm that cut the big superficial veins. But somebody, a cop I think, slapped a tourniquet on him and got him to the hospital. We sewed him up and gave him plasma and whole blood—he got a pint of mine—and smugly waited for him to wake up. He did, and he was nuts. Incoherent, disoriented. At that point I tottered off to home and bed.

"When I came in on Wednesday afternoon, they had him transferred from surgery to psycho. Lieutenant Borovsky's in charge of psycho, but I don't think you have to know very much to handle a psycho ward Russian style. They have something they call 'sleep therapy.' This means you give the patient a twenty-four-hour shot of barbiturate. If he's still nuts when he wakes up, you give him another one, and so on. Maybe there are angles to it that I don't understand, but Borovsky's English isn't any better than my Russian.

"I'd asked around during the day and found out what happened to Gribble. He was a stranger in town and he turned up at Clapp's Department Store. He bought a pair of socks and a salesgirl noticed him standing around for maybe ten minutes inside, hanging back from the revolving door. The side doors were locked, and nuts to the fire laws. Clapp's doesn't aim to air-condition the whole town. Well, she's seen eighty-year-old farmwomen do exactly the same thing, but she thought it was awfully funny for a middle-aged man. Finally Gribble made the plunge into the revolving door, and naturally it stuck half-way. The wooden tip from somebody's umbrella jammed it. Gribble began screaming and pounding and in no time at all he had the glass smashed and his arm cut up. So they toted him away and the salesgirl said Mr. Clapp was *livid* because his plate-glass insurance is all whacked up by this new insurance-company consolidation that nobody seems to be able to collect from and also he had to open the side doors and turn off his precious air conditioning.

"So much for that. I looked at Gribble's papers in the hospital office. He's a machine-shop setup man from Scranton. He was released as surplus last week by the Erie. He got a travel permit good to Corning to look for a job there. His hobbies are baseball, bowling, and fishing. He belongs to the American Federation of Machinists, the Red Cross, and the Veterans of Foreign Wars. Normal?"

"Normal," Justin said.

"Phony. Because I went to see him in psycho. He was just coming out of his first twenty-four-hour-sleep. Mumbling and stirring. Then the mumbling got clearer. Gribble the normal machinist was reciting Moliere in the original. As far as I could judge, his accent was very good. It was Act Two of *Le Misanthrope*. He seemed to be enjoying himself."

"Come on," Justin said. "It happens every day. He heard the Moliere once, maybe when he was a child, and it stayed in his sub-conscious. Under drugs—"

"Naturally," Betsy said, very cool and composed. "And tell me, doctor: when and where in his childhood did he hear the order of battle of the Red Armies as of April 17?"

"No," Justin said defensively.

"Yes. I don't remember it all, but after the Moliere his face changed and he began to mutter the date. Then he began to rattle off the armies, the corps, the divisions. With commanders' names and locations around El Paso. Map-grid locations. He was just swinging into 'Appreciation and Development of Combat Situation, for Eyes of Combined Chiefs of Staff Only' when Borovsky came strutting down the ward.

"He beamed down at Gribble, the normal machinist, who by then was massing a Canadian Army Group, the 17th, I think, for a spoiling attack on the left flank of the Red bulge. 'Patient motch batter,' Borovsky said, and on he went. His English is 99 per cent bluff, thank the Lord. But the night-duty officer was Major Lange and I had to shut Gribble up before his inspection. He really talks it. I finally slapped Gribble awake and he began to cry.

"'Pull yourself together,' I told him. 'You've been talking about the wrong things in your sleep. They'll give you another shot if they don't think you're better. You're in the Chiunga General Hospital. Tell 'em you're just nervous and tired. They *want* to get minor cases out of here if they can. Play along with them. Fit into the routine and you'll be out of here fast.'

"He understood me, the scared little guy. I don't know what kind of personal hell he was going through, but I could *see* him pushing it away, hard, with every muscle. 'Fit into the routine,' he said at last. 'This is the Chiunga General Hospital. I'm Gribble. I just got panicky stuck in the—that place. I'm better now. Just tired and nervous.' Hysteria kept trying to break in between the words. And he wouldn't let it.

"'Great,' I told him. 'Stay on the rails. Here they come.' Borovsky was leading Lange through the ward. When they stopped at Gribble's bed, Lange asked me what the devil I was doing there. Told him I might be able to expedite the discharge of Mr. Gribble.

"'Discharge? What are you talking about? This man is seriously ill.'

"Gribble spoke up then, bless him. 'I don't *think* I am, sir,' he said apologetically. 'I know I blanked out, but I feel all right now. Just a little nervous and tired.' They didn't notice that he had his eyes on me through it—I think that helped him.

"'Patient motch batter,' that pompous ass Borovsky said.

"Lange put him through the questioning. Gribble knew who he was and where he was and why he was there. Then there was a good deal of Russian between Lange and Borovsky, and then the major said to me: 'It seems you were correct. He should not be in one of our beds. Have the clerical section arrange for outpatient status and board with some responsible family.'

"That wasn't quite what I'd hoped for, but

then I thought of you." She came to a dead stop.

Billy Justin said slowly: "How long would he be on my neck?"

"Until he's discharged. Comparable cases have been discharged after two checkup visits—call it a month."

"Who do you suppose he is, Betsy?"

"I don't know. I can't imagine. He wasn't any government official up top; I know most of the faces. He couldn't possibly be a field commander. Our Mr. Gribble would never rise to corporal in the field army. He's some kind of planner, maybe a Pentagon colonel, though that doesn't seem right either. Whoever he is, he's had a shock that almost broke him. He's a brave little man. And they'll shoot him if they find out that he isn't who he claims to be."

"He isn't the only one they'll shoot," Justin said. She made some kind of reply and he shouted at her: "All right. I'll be the responsible family. I'll be his mother and his father and his goddamned old aunt Tissie." She raised one hand feebly as he spewed his rage at her. "Send him along! Dump him here. You knew I couldn't turn you down. Even if I thought I closed the books in Korea. Even if I've been wasting the best years of my life as a peasant. Billy's a patriot, you can always count on him. You think it's a game. You live in a white house on the hill and you've never been shot. You never lay in a field hospital with an infected wound eating your leg off; you never screamed when you saw them coming with the needle for your fifteenth penicillin shot in two days. You think it's a game. So send your brave little man along, I'll take care of him. But after what you've done, don't ever speak to me again."

He turned from her stunned white face and limped down the hill.

CHAPTER SIX

Two Russian medics delivered Gribble the next afternoon. They looked about in a puzzled way and kept asking: *"Sooproogah? Seen? Donkh?"* Justin supposed they were wondering about the rest of the responsible family. "I don't understand," he told them, dead pan. Finally there was the receipt to sign and they drove away, still with the puzzled air.

"You're Gribble," Justin said to the little man. He was trembling under the hot sun. He nodded and gave a frightened glance at the house.

Justin, through an almost sleepless night, had decided on his approach. If the man wanted to be Gribble the machinist, then

Gribble the machinist he would be. Justin wanted no confidences. Justin wanted Gribble to be a nervous-breakdown outpatient and nothing more. He also wanted the two medics to report that fermer Yoostin had no family and that patient Gribble should therefore be placed somewhere else, but he doubted that they would go so far.

"Ever done any farming?"

"No."

"Ever have a little vegetable garden?"

"Yes. Oh yes. I've done that."

"Good. Well, I'll show you your room." He started for the house, Gribble lagging behind. When Justin entered the kitchen, he was climbing the two steps to the porch. And there he stood, before the screen door, with the look on his face of a man who has seen a cobra.

"Come on in," Justin said through the door.

"I'd rather not unless I have to, Mr. Justin," came from that mask of terror.

Justin remembered that his blowup had occurred when he was trapped in a revolving door. And he was also wearily conscious of the endless petty inconveniences that would nag him if Gribble balked at every doorway.

"Nothing's going to happen to you, Gribble," he said with an edge on his voice. "It's a perfectly ordinary fly-blown slummy bachelor's kitchen." The man smiled meagerly. Justin held the door open and waited; Gribble stepped convulsively over the threshold, closing his eyes for a moment. Justin closed the door quietly on Gribble's rigid back; instinct told him that to let it slam in its normal violent fashion would immediately involve him in a pack of trouble.

"Sit down and have some coffee," he told the little man. Coffee was not casually drunk these days. If you had it, you saved it for a good jolt in the morning. But he *had* to make this man relax; otherwise life would be an unbearable round of walking on eggs.

Gribble sat and said "Thank you" into his steaming cup.

"It isn't such a bad life here," Justin said tentatively. "I think you'll eat a little better than you would in town. You can hold back eggs and hide your chickens when they come around. And the work won't be too hard with the two of us. Hell, wherever you are you have to work—it might as well be here."

"That's right," said Gribble eagerly.

The conversation then petered out. They finished their coffee and Justin led the way to the porch. "The barn needs cleaning out," he said. "I'll show you where the—" He stopped. Gribble stood inside the kitchen and he outside, the screen door between them.

Justin sighed and held the door open for the little man. With an apologetic smile Gribble lunged through the doorway, eyes shut for a moment.

So it went through the afternoon. Gribble walked willingly into the barn and worked hard, but when Justin sent him to the tool shed built on the house for a trenching spade he was gone ten minutes. Justin went after him, swearing. It was, of course, the tool-shed door. Gribble was reaching for the handle, but he couldn't quite bring himself to touch it.

Justin opened the door grimly, yanked out the spade, handed it to Gribble, and closed the door. His resolution to let Gribble be Gribble cracked wide open. "What is all this?" he demanded.

The little man said faintly: "I had a very disagreeable experience once. Very disagreeable." He leaned against the toolshed wall, his face white. "I'd rather not discuss it."

Justin, alarmed, said: "All right. We won't. Let's get back to the barn—if you can make it?"

Gribble could make it. He worked through to dinnertime, hard and well. Justin cooked a wretched bachelor's meal big enough for two and held the door for Gribble to come in and eat. He didn't eat much; something was on his mind. He finally asked if he could have a cot on the porch instead of a bedroom.

"Sure," said Justin. "I'll get a cot from the attic." And to himself: I might have expected it.

After dinner they had three hours of light and used it to haul water from the spring up the road to the tank in the cow barn. When he did the job himself, he could use nothing but a pair of galvanized pails. Gribble's help meant that between them they could fill a hundred-pound milk can on each trip. Justin began to feel a little more optimistic about meeting the brutal new milk norm. Each of his cows would, for the first time since the pasture spring went dry in June, get all the water she wanted that night. In his cheerfulness he scarcely noticed Gribble except as the hand on the other handle of the hundred-pound can. But when they topped off the tank with their twenty-fourth load, an exhausted voice asked him: "Is there more to do?"

Gribble was on the verge of collapse. "My God," Justin said, "I'm sorry. You're out of the hospital—I didn't think. Cows come first," he added bitterly. "Sure, we can knock off. I'll get that cot."

The little man slumped on the porch steps while he set it up in the gathering darkness and then without a word fell onto the dusty canvas. He was asleep in seconds. Justin thought, went for a cotton blanket, and spread it over Gribble to keep the flies off his face and hands and went to the road for a final smoke before turning in. There was a sawed-off tree stump he usually sat on where you could watch the sunset.

Rawson was waiting there. "Hi, Billy," the legless man said easily.

"Hello." Justin had his pouch out. Grudgingly he held it to Rawson. "Smoke?"

"Thanks." Rawson whisked a single cigarette paper from his breast pocket, dipped thumb and finger in the pouch. In a twirl and a lick he had a cigarette made. *A tramp*, Justin thought. *A drifting bum with all the skills of a drifting bum. How easily he takes it! What's it to him that he's a drifter under the Reds or the United States? A perennial outlaw—and God, how I envy his peace of mind!* Heavily he stuffed his pipe with dry tobacco. Rawson had lit his cigarette and politely passed him the burning match. He puffed the pipe alight. It tasted vile, but it was tobacco.

Rawson was inhaling luxuriously. "Not bad," he commented. "Your own stuff?"

"About half. The rest is from Croley. There was a tax stamp on it, but I think it's local stuff too. He probably refilled a pack with some junk he bought from a farmer."

"My, such goings on from the virtuous storekeeper. Well, I brought that package. A man'll be by tonight or tomorrow."

"Well, let's see it."

Rawson reached deep into the "boot" of his gocart, a space where his legs would have fitted if he'd had any. The package was small and dim in the fading light.

The set of his muscles, the leverage of his arm should have warned Justin to brace himself when the package was handed over, but he was disarmed by the smallness of the thing. He took the package, found it amazingly heavy, fumbled it for a moment, and dropped it, almost on his toe. It sank an inch into the not particularly soft ground.

"Oops!" Rawson said apologetically. "I should have warned you it was heavy."

"Yes," Justin said. "And maybe you should have warned me it was an atomic bomb."

"Just part of one," Rawson said.

"You know Betsy Cardew?" Justin asked, looking at the package by his toe, wondering vaguely about radioactivity, wondering whether he ought to move his toe.

"Of course. Mailwoman."

"Are you and she in this together?"

"In what?" Rawson asked blandly.

"We are not amused, Rawson. This thing—"

He choked. "I got beautifully mad at her. I'm still sore. I think she's a silly kid who had no right to get me involved. You—you know the score. So—why me, Rawson? *Why me?*"

The legless man said brutally: "If you think I'm going to flatter you, you're going to be disappointed. It's you, Justin, because we're scraping the bottom of the barrel. Our best and bravest are in Siberian labor camps now, or mining uranium in the Antarctic. Why *you*, indeed! Have I got any business scooting around after dark with a suitcase bomb in my lap?"

"But what's it all for?" Justin almost begged. "What can we do? Suitcase bombs, yes, but then what?"

"That," Rawson said, "is none of your business, as a moment of thought will convince you. Will you handle the transfer or won't you?"

"I will," Justin said bitterly. "Thanks for your confidence in me. I hope it's well placed."

"So do I, Justin. So do I. Will you push me off?"

He went creaking down the road.

Justin relit his pipe and studied the dying sunset. Then he picked up the heavy little package, walked to the barn, and hid it behind a bale of hay. It was not very well hidden. He wanted to be able to get it fast and get it off his hands fast. Furthermore, he knew very well that no amount of energy spent in hiding unshielded uranium or plutonium would safeguard it against search with a scintillation counter.

He stepped quietly past Gribble, sleeping on the porch, and went upstairs to his bedroom. He did not intend to sleep that night—not while waiting for an unknown person to pick up an atomic-bomb subassembly for use in some insane, foredoomed scheme of sabotage.

He tried to read but could not. He smoked the last of his tobacco in two unwanted pipefuls.

Insane, the whole business! There were supposed to be 5 million occupation troops east of the Mississippi alone. Their own third-rate shopping place, Chiunga Center, was garrisoned by the 449th Soviet Military Government Unit, which, when administrative transport and medical frills were ripped off, turned out to be a reinforced infantry regiment: about one thousand fighting men armed to the teeth.

And what could you do?

Well, you could denounce Rawson and turn his bomb over to the 449th SMGU. You could denounce Betsy Cardew—nit-witted rich girl who used sex and your vestigial pride to unload a deadly menace on you. You could get written up as a patriotic citizen of the North American People's Democratic Republic, get a life pension as a Hero of Socialist Labor. And then there would be nothing for you to do but cut your throat in self-loathing.

In spite of himself he fell asleep at 3:00 A.M., with the 40-watt bulb shining on his face and the unread book open across his chest.

CHAPTER SEVEN

He woke with a panicky start at eight-thirty. What was wrong? Something was terribly wrong.

At the window he saw the cows turned out to pasture. But they should have been bellowing, unmilked, for an hour or more—

But the milk cans were stacked on the loading platform for the pickup truck. Gribble had milked them! With only a few words from yesterday afternoon to go on he had worked the milking machine and turned the cows out.

And that meant he had been in the barn, where—

Justin dashed downstairs, his heart thudding, and then slowed deliberately to a walk. He found the little man in the yard before the barn scouring the milker and pails. "Good morning," he said.

"Good morning, Mr. Justin. I don't know if I did the right thing, but the cows were stamping around and I remembered what you told me—it wasn't hard."

"You did exactly the right thing. I couldn't get to sleep last night. And when I did, I guess I couldn't wake up. I'm sorry I left it all to you. Have you been in the—kitchen?"

Gribble smiled nervously and shook his head.

"I'll fix breakfast."

Justin kept himself, by an effort of will, from walking into the barn, in plain sight of Gribble, and looking to see whether that bale of hay had been disturbed. He turned to the house, started the stove, and cooked oatmeal. Half a pint of withheld butterfat made oatmeal breakfast enough for a morning's hard work. When it was cooked, he called Gribble, who stopped on the porch apologetically until the door was held open for him.

They ate silently.

"Mind washing up?" Justin asked at last. "I'll be working in the kitchen garden." As he left, he latched back the screen door, feeling like a fool.

He was heading not for the garden but for the barn when the chug of a worn-out truck sounded along his road. It was Milkshed arriving ahead of time, he absently supposed, and went over to the loading deck to give a hand with the cans. But it wasn't the Milkshed truck that rounded the turn. It was a worn blue panel job throbbing and groaning out of all proportion to its size. On the near panel was lettered: *Bee-Jay Farm Supplies and Machinery, Washington, Penna.*

It stopped by the milk cans and a nondescript driver leaned out. "This the Justin place?"

"Yes. I'm Justin. You have anything for sale, mister?"

"Might let you have some plastic pipe."

"Got an electric pump to go with it? My spring's downhill from the barn."

"Yes, I guess I passed it. Sorry about the pump, but we don't have them yet. Maybe by next spring, the way things are going."

"That's good to hear. You know you're the first salesman I've seen here in three years?"

"That's what they all say. Bee-Jay's an enterprising outfit. We got the first A-440 passes in the state. Say, are you by any chance a friend of Rawson's?"

Justin knew then who he was. "I know him," he said. "I guess I shouldn't take the pipe if I can't use it right away. Seen Rawson lately?"

"I heard he was somewhere around here. He didn't happen to leave anything for me, did he?"

"Just a minute." He went to the barn aware that this was the moment of decision. There was no reason why Rawson and Betsy *couldn't* be framing him. There was no reason why Gribble *couldn't* be a planted witness for corroboration. The heavy package was behind the bale of hay where he had put it in darkness. He couldn't possibly know whether Gribble had found it and replaced it or not. And now, picking it up, carrying it, handing it silently to the man in the truck, he had completed his treason to the North American People's Democratic Republic. He had received, harbored, and transmitted fissionable material. His head was in the noose from that moment on.

He felt all the better for it.

"Good old Rawson," the Bee-Jay man chuckled, hefting the package. "Well, Mr. Justin, I'll try to pass by again—with a pump."

"Do that," Justin said steadily. "And if you ever feel any need to call on me, do it. I'm available. For anything."

The man smiled blandly. The starting motor cranked and strained for fifteen seconds before the engine caught and the little truck lurched off down the road. Justin followed it with his eyes until it was over the next crest and out of sight.

He turned to find Gribble staring at him from the corner of the barn. Justin wasn't frightened; the time for that was past. He realized that he would feel physical fear before long while he waited in some schoolhouse cellar for the MVD to come clumping in with truncheons and methodically reduce him to a blob of pain, shrieking confessions on demand. But he did not fear the fear to come.

He told Gribble easily: "The first salesman in three years. He had some pipe but he didn't have a pump. Maybe by spring, he said. I guess things are picking up all around."

"Yes," Gribble said vaguely, his eyes full of tears.

They worked steadily through the morning and afternoon. Gribble spent two hours on the milk cooler, which had been grunting, gurgling, and creaking for a month, on the verge of a breakdown. Whatever else he was besides—quoter of Moliere, Pentagon colonel—he was unquestionably an able refrigeration mechanic and bench hand. He serviced the motor and coils, disassembled the pump, cut new gaskets from a discarded inner tube, filed a new cam from scrap metal and installed it. The cooler whispered happily and the red line of the thermometer dropped well below the danger mark for the first time that summer. He showed Justin his work, dimly proud, and then joined him in culti-vating the knee-high field corn until it was time to haul water from the spring again. They had a late supper at three-thirty: a dubious piece of boiled salt pork, potatoes from the barrel in the cellar, milk. It was then that Gribble asked whether Justin happened to have anything to drink.

"Some local brandy," Justin said, wondering. The little man was tightening up again. If you were an artist you saw him as taut cords vibrating in the shape of a human body. He had seemed almost happy and slack when he showed Justin the cooler . . . .

"Could I please—?"

Justin got the carelessly hidden bottle of Mr.

Konreid's popskull. Gribble methodically poured himself half a tumblerful, not bothering to rinse his glass of its skim of rich milk. Methodically he drank it down, his Adam's apple working. "Rotten stuff," he said after a long pause. Justin was about to be offended when he somehow realized that Gribble didn't mean his liquor in particular. "I was partly tanked when I had that trouble in the—department store." The taut strings were relaxing a little. "But sometimes you haven't got anything else and you have to get to sleep."

Uninvited, he refilled his tumbler to the halfway mark. Justin protested: "Man, what's the good of getting drunk in the afternoon? We have another milking and the corner fence post is sagging; that'll take both of us to fix. Pour that back in the bottle, will you? You can have it after supper if you can't sleep."

Gribble methodically drank it down. "No point in fooling around," the little man said gravely. "You pretend you're somebody else, fine. But you know you aren't, especially when you're trying to sleep. You're still the fellow who closed the door. But that was only half the job, Justin. Funny part is if you do the first half—that is if you're a fellow like me—then you can't do the second half. They never thought of that. I must have looked pretty good on the profile. Hard-bitten, waspish executive and all that. But I didn't fool the combat boys. I went right out of Prudential—you should have seen my office, Justin!—and right into the Pentagon. I told them—what do you say?—I told them: 'Alert, capable executive desires connection with first-class fighting force. Feels his abilities are not being used to the utmost capacity in present employment.' I went through the lieutenants and captains like a hot knife through butter. I've handled kids like that all my life. G-1 checked me through. You know why? Because G-1's just office management in uniform. We talked the same language. I was exactly like them so they thought I was *good*. So I got my appointment with Clardy. Three stars. Colonel Hagen—imagine having a chicken colonel for a *secretary*—Hagen briefed him first, told him I was talent, hard-boiled talent, kind of talent they needed fast for a battalion, then a regiment, then maybe a division. You go up fast in wartime if you've got the stuff. So Clardy talked to me for a few minutes and then he turned to Hagen. As if I wasn't there. Cussed Hagen out for wasting his time. 'Good Lord, Colonel, get him something in G-1 or G-4, but don't ever give him a combat command. Look at him! Can you imagine *him* committing troops?'

"You see, Justin? He was on to me in two minutes. They never say it, even among themselves, but they know combat command doesn't take brains. They talk about brilliant field generals, but when you try to find out what the brilliance was it's always this: G-1 gets the brilliant general his men; G-2 gets the brilliant general his information, G-3 trains the men and plans the attack, G-4 gets the supplies. Then the brilliant general says

'Attack!' and it's another victory.

"You know, you don't need brains to say 'Attack!' Plenty of them have brains and they don't seem to do them any damage, but brains aren't essential. What you need's character. When you've got character, you say 'Attack!' at the right time. And Clardy saw in two minutes that I didn't have it. That I'd wait and hang back and try to think of ways around when there aren't any ways around at all. That when G-3 told me it was time to attack I wouldn't take his word for it, I'd hem and haw and wonder if he really believed what he was telling me. Clardy saw clean through me, Justin. I'm a man who can cheerfully commit a battery of IBM card punches to the fray and that's all."

The little man lurched to his feet and stared, red-eyed, at Justin. Waiting.

Slowly and unwillingly Justin said: "What do you want, Gribble? What am I supposed to do about all this?"

Staring, Gribble said: "Very cagey, Justin. But you've got to help me. I know you're committed. I milked the cows this morning. I'm a picture straightener; I always have been. So I started to straighten that bale of hay. Package behind it—heavy package. So heavy it's got to be gold or lead or plutonium. And I know it isn't gold or lead.

"The farm salesman came by. I looked in the barn—no package. You're in it, Justin. You've got to help me. I can't help myself. Five thousand of them! And then, of course, I couldn't pull the second half of the job. Clardy was right . . . ."

He stood up, swaying a little. "Come along, Justin. You've got to do something for me."

Gribble lurched through the doorway, past the latched-back screen door, down the cement walk to the road.

Justin followed slowly. "It's about fifteen miles," Gribble said over his shoulder.

I've got to go along, Justin told himself. The little man's guessed—and he's right—that I'm a traitor to the People's Democratic Republic. He might tell anybody if it takes his fancy. Perhaps, he bleakly thought, I'll have to kill him. Meanwhile he doesn't get out of my sight.

"What do you want me to do, exactly?" he asked Gribble in a calm, reasonable voice.

The little man said abruptly: "Open a door."

CHAPTER EIGHT

They walked for two hours, Gribble in the lead and mumbling.

Justin tried at first to get him to make sense, then to at least accept a cover story. "We're going to Bert Loughlin's about a calf, Gribble. O.K.? Will you tell them that if we get stopped? Bert Loughlin's about a calf—"

"Ghosts," Gribble said, preoccupied.

Six miles along the road, they were overtaken by a wagon, Eino Baaras at the reins. He was returning from Clayboro to Glencairn—"Little Finland"—with locust poles. He scowled at them and offered a ride.

"Thanks," Gribble said. "We're going to see Bert Loughlin about a calf."

Baaras shrugged and waited for them to get

up before he said: "Loughlin ain't got no calf."
He touched up the team and the wagon rolled.

"Selling, not buying," Justin said.

"Loughlin ain't got no money," Baaras said
unconcernedly.

"Maybe something to swap," Justin said.
He was clenching his fists. What came next?
*Loughlin ain't got nothing to swap. Where you
really headed, Yustin?* But Baaras just dipped
some snuff, spat into the dust, and said
nothing.

Silent Finns, Justin thought suddenly,
drowsy with the afternoon heat. Worse for
them than for us. They've been followed
halfway around the world by the neighbors
they fled while we sat and waited and perhaps
were happy in our blindness . . . .

He dozed for a while; Gribble shook him
awake. "We get off here, Mr. Justin." The
wagon had stopped and Baaras was sardoni-
cally waiting.

"Thanks," he said to the Finn, and looked
uncertainly at Gribble for a lead. The little
man started up a rutted and inconsiderable
wagon track that angled from the blacktop.
Justin followed him, disoriented for a
moment. Then he realized that they were on
the west side of Prospect Hill and heading up
it.

Baaras looked at them, shrugged, and drove
on. Justin thought flatly: A *total* botch. I said
the wrong thing, we got off at the wrong place.
I couldn't have botched it worse if I'd been
waving a flag with TRAITOR embroidered on
it. The only thing to do now is wait and hope.

Baaras is going to talk about my peculiar goings on, and the people he talks to will talk. Eventually it'll get to somebody like Croley and that means I'm dead.

Meanwhile you keep climbing Prospect Hill.

The Hill was about 2,500 feet high and heavily wooded. It was supposed to be owned by one of the great New York real-estate fortunes. Farmers who tried to buy some small pieces adjoining their fields for woodlots were rebuffed. A fair-sized local mutual insurance company which tried once to buy a big piece for development got an interview in New York City and a courteous explanation that the Hill was being held against the possibility that the area would experience major growth. The president of the company considered that interview one of the high points of his life, and Justin had heard all about it. So had practically everybody who'd spent ten minutes with the president.

The Hill was posted against hunting and fishing, but not fenced in. Farmers around it had more or less fenced it out with their own wire, but there were gaps like the one Gribble had found. Kids and hunters stayed clear of the Hill for the most part. Among the kids there was a legend that the Vanderbilts—or was it the Astors?—would jail you for twenty years if you got caught trespassing. And the hunters knew that the Hill had no springs and only one intermittent stream. It was against local custom to carry a canteen for a day's hunting; you were heavily joshed for dressing up like a Boy Scout. So you pretty much stayed away—

But what wheels had worn the twin ruts up the Hill?

Justin kicked at an angle of crushed rock. It should have flown up and away from the loose gravel it was embedded in and Justin should have strode on feeling infinitesimally better for the release of tension. It didn't happen that way at all. The rock stayed where it was and blinding pain shot through Justin's foot. While he stopped and swore, Gribble turned. "Wasting time," he said mildly.

"In a minute," Justin said. The pain was dying down, but he wasn't ready to go on walking. He stooped and tried to wiggle the fang of rock protruding from the gravel, work it loose, and throw it away. It had wounded him and it must surely die.

The rock wouldn't wiggle. Evidently it was a protruding corner of a really big chunk. He pawed at the loose gravel to investigate. It wasn't loose gravel. His fingers skidded over the surface without disordering a single one of the round and oval glacier-ground stones.

"Come on," Gribble said impatiently, and resumed climbing. Justin followed thoughtfully. The rutted, worn secondary road, this road that was clearly on the very verge of breaking up, was a very remarkable road indeed. It looked bad. It *was* bad. It would give the springs of a truck a very hard time.

But it would never get worse. It would never break up. It was a good road disguised as a bad one. Reinforced concrete a yard down, no doubt. On top of that the crushed rock and gravel mortared into position. A heavy-duty highway that would pass air reconnaissance and even a ground patrol.

"Yes, yes, yes," Gribble was muttering ahead of him.

A heavy-duty highway to where?

"Gribble," he said.

The small man turned on him in fury. His voice was an almost womanish screech. "Leave me alone, Justin! Don't distract me. This thing's hard enough without you yammering and yipping at my heels. I'm fighting with myself to keep from turning around and running down the hill. I could break down right now if I let go. I could have a fine time crying and kicking and screaming and letting the clouds close in on what I have to do. But—I—won't. *Shut up and follow me!*"

Justin followed, confused and burning with resentment. He had been in contact with psychopaths before and, as now, it was never pleasant. A girl in the ad agency, years ago, at the next drawing table to his, took six months to go thoroughly insane, a little more each day. Toward the end there were worried conferences behind her back, long wrangles about when eccentricity slips over into mania, and always the stolid, unimaginative conferee who spoke what was in everybody's mind: "All she has to do is get hold of herself; she doesn't *have* to act like a nut." Naturally in the age of Freud no really informed person spoke those words; naturally you were shocked to hear them. But oh, the resentment that filled you when you had to humor and defer to and make your life miserable because of a crackpot!

A faded sign nailed to a tree pointed up the peculiar road: PROSPECT VISTA, it said, which made no sense at all. A prospect is a vista and a vista is a prospect. Justin could have said something about it but dared not, bullied into silence by the little man who wouldn't control himself.

The road shot suddenly upward and ended at a big, littered clearing. The litter was the debris of a housing development that had never come to pass. Justin never knew it was there. This was Prospect Vista, a big rain-dimmed sign said. Below, in smaller letters, the sign announced split-level homes, no down payment, seventy dollars a month, pay like rent.

Bulldozers had been at work tearing out trees and piling them like jackstraws. Dirt streaks had been hoed out of the forest duff long ago—long enough for underbrush and scrub to spring up again in barbed-wire tangles. The bulldozed roads-to-be were now more impassable than they had been before the bulldozers came. But hopeful signs marked them: Onondaga Avenue intersected Seneca Street where they stood on the clearing's edge.

Sewer trenches were dug clear down to hardpan, an elephantine checkerboard converging on the principal landmark of Prospect Vista, which was a huge hole, obviously the excavation for a treatment plant. And that was as far as things had got. Here and there was a load of rusty pipe or pencil rod to reinforce concrete that had never been poured. Gravel and sand stood in low cones dotted through the clearing. In the years that passed, they had found their angle of repose and would slump no lower. It occurred to Justin that one pile of gravel may be alive and another dead. These were dead.

Gribble was saying suddenly in a tone of sweet reasonableness: "Of course, I wasn't in on the planning end. I came in fairly late, after Clardy turned me down for a command. But you can guess how they put it together. The techniques the Scandinavians developed, plus the brute-force Manhattan District idea plus a security plan borrowed from the Japanese and improved on by the supply system of the Czarist Army. The one that kept losing them all their wars."

As he spoke, he moved up and down a few yards of the steeply inclined end of the road like a hound trying to pick up a scent. Now and then he knelt and fingered a stone.

"All that planning," he chattered, "and then in a weak moment they turned it over to me. A fuzzy-faced West Point second-classman would have been better, of course. I was supposed to be a hard guy. Once I signed orders for a 20 per cent firing effective Christmas Eve. Deliberately, to make the surviving 80 percent cringe a little. But there's a difference—"

He had found whatever he was looking for.

"Lift here," he told Justin, indicating two shards of concrete that projected from the good-bad road. His face was deathly pale.

Justin hadn't been listening. He had been thinking: *A total breakdown. He's completely irresponsible, in a dream world. He's likely to say anything to anybody. Perhaps I ought to pick up one of those reinforcing rods over there and—*

"What's that?" he asked the little man.

Gribble patiently repeated, "Lift here," and showed him the hunks of concrete.

Murder was on Justin's mind. "Stand over there," he said sharply. He wasn't to be caught bending over with the lunatic behind him and reinforcing rods conveniently near. Gribble, pale and exhausted, stood where he pointed, yards away, and nevertheless, Justin watched him as he heaved on the shards. Because of that he missed seeing the miracle, but he felt its weight through his back and shoulder muscles and heard its creak and hum.

A great slab of the good-bad road came up like a door, twelve feet wide, easily twenty feet long. He crazily thought at first that he had pried it up with his fingers, and then he heard a motor and the whine of a gearbox.

Justin leaped back and the hinged slab continued to rise. It was a yard thick, supported on I beams.

To where?

The good-bad road ended at the gateway to a tunnel angling sharply down. At the gateway the masquerade ended. The tunnel flooring was plain concrete. Lights had gone on, one every couple of yards along the ceiling. He had a confused impression of huge counter-weights moving down as the slab moved up, and then motion stopped; the tunnel lay open.

Gribble's voice penetrated his stupor. "Come on, Justin. Inside." He stepped in and let Gribble show him a lever, which he pulled, and which lowered the ponderous slab down on them again. He let Gribble, stammering and sweating, lead him a hundred feet down the inclined tunnel to a huge door, to Justin's eyes exactly like that of a bank vault.

"That's it," Gribble said, his voice charged with poisonous self-hatred. "Open it, Justin."

CHAPTER NINE

The artist stammered a question about the combination. Gribble whispered: "No combination. Just that lever."

No—it wasn't like a bank vault's door after all. There was just the one lever. This door was meant to open easily. From the outside.

Justin turned the lever and pulled. The door glided open and starved concentration-camp corpses tumbled out into the tunnel. Justin leaped back; his own scream of horror yelled back at him, reverberating along the tunnel's smooth walls.

He was turning to run blindly back when Gribble took his arm. "Look at them," Gribble said softly. "There was no pain. I was never sure of that. Naturally I was told it would be painless, but they'd tell me that anyway. But it was true. They never knew what hit them, Justin. I feel just a little better now."

Justin finally forced himself to look. There was no distortion of agony on the faces; they were people who had gone to sleep and never wakened. He became conscious of a cool, dry, gentle draft from the open doorway. "Pseudo mummies," Gribble said. "You find them in high, dry places. The Andes, the Iranian upland." He looked earnestly into one of the calm faces. "Dr. Swenson. A very good man. I suppose he guessed what had happened, got a few people together, and went to work on the door. Quietly—no panic."

The dry, brown hand of the man he looked down at was cramped around the twin pipe of an oxyacetylene torch. Another pair of dry brown arms held cylinders of gas. Another had been straightening a kinked tube when time became eternity.

"No panic," Gribble mused. "His watchword used to be 'Step back and take a long, calm look.' He kept us together after the polio epidemic. I for one was ready to yell for help. 'Step back,' he said, and I did and we decided we could swing it as we were. That Swenson. He felt the air go cold and dry, he figured it out, he got his men together, they got to work on the door. And then the gas came. Without pain."

All Justin could make of it was that Gribble had killed—or thought he had killed—some people beyond the door. "Tell me about it," he said calmly.

"I'll show you," said the little man. "After all, it's your baby now. I couldn't be expected to go on with it now, could I? *Could I?*" His eyes were wild.

"Of course not," Justin said very steadily. "You just show me what you have to and don't worry. I'll see that the right thing's done."

"Come on," Gribble said.

They stepped around the bodies and through the door. Into a garage. The little man absently went from wall to wall turning on lights. It was quite a place, and it was crowded with servicing equipment and trucks. No two trucks were built alike, painted alike, or marked alike. Some of them Justin vaguely recognized. There was the two-ton stake-bed job, very battered, marked *P. DiPumpo & Sons, Contractors*. He had absent-mindedly registered the odd name a few times during the past few years. The battered truck of P. DiPumpo & Sons had intersected his orbit on the highway, or in town, or perhaps during the early months of the war passing his farm. Trucks came and went.

A half-ton cab-over-engine job: *Hornell Florists*.

A huge, ordinary, bright-red gas truck: *Supeco Refining Company*.

A tractor-trailer job, special trailer with the bed sunk between the axles: *U. S. Bridge Building Corporation*. He had seen that one, noticing the odd profile of a bulky load covered with roped tarpaulins.

Thirty more of them, reefers, pickups, vans, dumpers, tow cars—you name it and it was there. Two hundred feet under Prospect Hill was a haunted garage with dry, brown people sprawled here and there, as they would fall from timing an engine, cleaning spark plugs, turning down brake drums, and—in one small corner—stamping out counterfeit license plates for the year just past.

"Come on," Gribble said again.

He led Justin from the garage into a bewildering underground industrial complex. There were drafting rooms, with dry brown draftsmen slumped forward on their tables. Offices, foundries, machine shops, welding bays, sheet-metal shops, laboratories, and desiccated corpses everywhere. Gribble kept pausing to look into faces. Sometimes he would name a name; usually he would turn to Justin and ask shrilly whether it wasn't obvious that they had died painlessly and in peace. Justin assured him over and over again.

The living quarters, below the working level, were the same. Spartan cubicles tunneling deep into the hill—Justin guessed dazedly that there might be five thousand of them strung along twenty corridors radiating from a plaza. The library, the cafeterias, the gymnasium. Sun lamps there, of course. And brown figures sprawled on the board track that circled it.

"What was it?" he had been asking for some time now of the unhearing little man. "I can't help if I don't know what it was, Gribble."

The little man led the way up from the living quarters to a freight elevator on the manufacturing level. He jerked the starting cable and the platform rose slowly with them to a square of blackness in the roof. "The satellite," Gribble said. "The super gadget, the ultimate doohickey that was going to win the war and keep it won."

"The ghost satellite? It's lost, Gribble," Justin said evenly. "They overran it in the sweep North. Betsy Cardew told me about it."

Gribble looked at him scornfully. "Not that one, you bloody fool," he said. "This one. The *real* one."

The freight elevator passed through the square of blackness and lights went on in a huge domed chamber of rock. In the center of the chamber stood a towering, spidery structure. Even Justin's untrained eye could see that it was a three-step rocket. Even he could see that the third step was designed to circle the Earth as an artificial satellite. And that it was heavily armed with bomb-launching racks.

CHAPTER TEN

You're a well-read average man, thought
Billy Justin, so you're aware that the human
race is about to take its next giant step. It's a
pity that it takes a war to do it, but that seems
to be the way people are. British imperial
greed long ago caused a Mr. John Harrison to
fuse metallurgy, physics, and genius into the
first marine chronometer, by means of which
the captains of His Britannic Majesty's Navy
were able to find a not yet plundered island
twice in succession. Before that Signor
Tartaglia, under the necessity of battering
down medieval walls sheltering medieval
thugs for the benefit of Renaissance thugs
with Renaissance cannon, stole sine, cosine,
and tangent from the philosophers' toy chest

and gave them to the world for tools. You know it was war that put jigs and fixtures on our machine tools, which is to say mass production: muskets to sewing machines, washers, kitchenware, Grand Rapids furniture, and the American standard of living. And another put planes in the air. And another avalanched radar, atomic bombs, and the first crude spaceships on us. You knew, therefore, like everybody else, that the current war was going to bring real manned space flight at last, not a potshot up and a quick scurrying back down to the ground, but people *living* there and *fighting* there, and the first step was the anti-radar bombardment satellite *Yankee Doodle* a-building in the Southwest somewhere on the Colorado plateau. The marvelous satellite would circle the Earth like the eye of God, but improved by American ingenuity. It could see. It could not be seen in return, at least not once it got past the initial launch period. Its paint job was blacker than black, albedo zero. Its antiradar electronics blinded the enemy ABM sites, it radiated none of its internal heat for the infrared sensors to feel and leaked no microwaves to fuzz an enemy screen, and its thirty-eight pups were as elusive as their dam. And deadly. Their more than Jovian thunderbolts were to strike down not one sinner at a time but whole sinful cities and—if they didn't disperse into ineffectiveness—sinful army groups. It was going to be a harsh, just world for sinners when the satellite *Yankee Doodle* roared up to begin its swift circling of the heavens, troubled though the progress of its construction was by sabotage. Troubled though it was by paratroopers. And there wasn't a dry eye in the house when the radio told you how *Yankee Doodle* was steam-rollered by the fifty thousand death-or-glory Chinese fanatics, hopped up to the eyebrows, of Task Force Tsing. The announcer brokenly announced: "Our men and women fought to the end against the human sea that engulfed them. The last weak radio communication from the site announced that thermite and demolition bombs had been fired to utterly destroy all components of *Yankee Doodle* so that the fanatical barbarian invaders—"

"Not that one, you bloody fool. This one. The *real* one."

Billy Justin craned his neck to study the monster. Its nose was lost in the upper gloom of the chamber. He emitted a sound like a nervous giggle. "I never thought we were that smart," he breathed.

Gribble was very happy. This was the ultimate in the pleasurable game of giving away confidences. "It's nothing new," he said with elaborate casualness. "We suckered the Germans this way when we invaded Europe the last time. There was this army group, see, waiting in England to make the real attack on the pas de Calais. The Germans knew it; they knew Patton was in command, they intercepted the radio traffic of the army group every day. Orders, acknowledgments, rations, troop movements, supplies, personnel transfers. So they almost ignored the feint by Bradley on the Cotentin Peninsula; they held forty divisions ready to meet the real thrust by Patton's army group. When it was too late, they found out that Patton's army group consisted of Patton and a couple of hundred radio operators. By then Bradley had broken out and was chewing his way across France."

"It is—ready?" asked Justin.

"No." The little man squatted on the concrete. "I'll begin at the beginning. You've got to know it all anyway."

"Why?" Justin asked sharply.

Gribble screwed up his face and his eyes began to leak tears. "I thought you agreed," he said miserably. "Didn't you say you'd handle it? I'm shot, Justin! I can't take any more—" His voice was soaring into childish shrillness.

"All right," Justin said hastily. "All right. Don't worry about a thing. If I've got to, I've got to. Just tell me."

Gribble blew his nose and shuddered. Shrilly at first, then more easily, he said: "It hasn't got any name. It's a three-step anti-radar multiple-warheaded exotic-fueled bombardment satellite, and we just called it 'the ghost.' It has a fishbowl reactor for housekeeping current. It has a hydrophonics room in action now under sun lamps. It's built for two. The TV tape and film library includes fifty thousand movies and books. An all-transistor radio sending and receiving set will function for an estimated seventy-five years without requiring servicing. Efficient waste and water regenerators are patterned after those aboard our long-cruise atomic submarines. Up there you can see the bomb deck, which accounts for half the weight of the third stage, neglecting fuel. A radar-computer bomb sight is capable of directing missiles to any point on the Earth's surface; delivery within five square miles is guaranteed. The satellite is armed with thirty-six hydrogen bombs and two special cobalt-jacketed bombs. I don't know why I'm telling you all this. You must have been reading about it since you were in high school."

Justin nodded. He had. Sandwiched between do-it-yourself pieces in the mechanics magazines, sandwiched between boy-and-girl stories in the slicks. He had. Everybody had. And here it was.

"And the only other thing about it," sighed Gribble, "is that it cannot be seen, detected or tracked. Or, therefore, defended against."

He stretched out a finger and touched the flared base of the immense machine. "It began six years ago. That's when I went to Clardy and offered my services. That's when all those ads appeared everywhere for engineers, scientists, technicians, toolmakers, mechanics. Remember the deluge?"

He did. Suddenly the United States seemed to have been gripped by a terrible hunger for trained men. It was as if—as if they were being drained off the normal labor supply. He said as much.

"That's right. And we're the ones who drained them off. We recruited for a year.

Half the ads you saw during that time might have been genuine; the rest were ours. From that fall on they were all genuine, and believe me, the aircraft and electronics industries were desperate. We'd drained off five thousand of the best people in the country. I sat in hotel rooms—Mr. Simpson of Aero Research, Mr. Blair of Pasadena Electronics —and interviewed around the clock. So did fifty others. We boiled down 200,000 people to five thousand.

"All the final selections knew was, 'hard, interesting, remunerative work, draft-proof but with a spice of danger.' When our table of organizations was filled, we had the darnedest collection of specialists ever assembled, and practically every one of them could double in construction work and the rest could learn. We trucked them to Prospect Hill. The construction and excavating machinery was here. I made my little speech telling 'em they were dead for the duration to the outside world. No passes, no furloughs, no anything. You see, Justin, there were spies among them. Had to be. But what's wrong with a spy if he's a good worker and can't get word outside the project? My security boys shot four people who tried to sneak out in the first month, and after that nobody tried. Were they spies? I don't know. Or care. They'd been warned . . .

"Nobody brought supplies to us; we went for our own. With my boys riding along in the cabs of the trucks. There'd be a freight car at an abandoned factory siding, we'd transfer the load, and that was that. We were under canvas through the first winter, but the Hill was beginning to take shape. It was the best cave in the Northeast. We enlarged it, braced it, squared it up.

"They were wonderful boys and girls, Justin. I don't know how to tell you. You know what a 'count' means in prison? That's how we treated them. Work gangs of twenty, always, and my security people roving around with whistles and guns. Blow the whistle at a gang, everybody drops everything and comes to attention and then you count them. If it's nineteen or twenty-one you check. Immediately. Well, somehow they managed not to mind it. Maybe they were thinking of the pay checks piling up against their accounts, maybe they were worked too hard to care, but maybe they knew they were shock troops, too.

"The last of them was underground in less than a year. It was still primitive in here—camp cots, no privacy, lousy food. Three good men went violently insane. What could we do? We locked 'em up and our medics cared for them and one of them recovered. We started stockpiling structural members for the satellite that winter. By then they knew what they were working on. Terrific lift. And by then—well, it was a good thing we had a computer man who also happened to be an ordained minister. Yes, Justin, I didn't show you the nursery. I think I'm behaving very well, but the nursery would be just a little more than I could take . . ."

He began to cry silently. Justin got up and

walked the circuit of the huge ship's base. When he returned, Gribble was dry eyed. "We acquired more trucks at that point," the little man said precisely. "For one year we did very little but warehouse supplies. Between times we improved our living quarters and recreational facilities. The monotony of the work had a bad effect. There were fads for painting, sculpture, and intramural competitive sports. I had to crack down on the waste of time and became utterly unpopular, which I was used to. The little stenos back in my insurance days called me 'The Monster,' you know. Things took an upturn when actual construction of the satellite began.

"The next year something unusual happened. There was somebody in one of those freight cars at one of those sidings. They brought him to me. He was a CIA man, and he knew he'd never be able to leave until the operation was over one way or another. He had a message that was a little too hot for our code room since it involved code-room personnel as well as the rest of us. Luckily— or by design—he was a former cafeteria manager, and was responsible for a great improvement in our mess. But the message, the message—when I decoded it in my own quarters I laughed and said: 'Melodrama.' And I went ahead and obeyed it. It was to install, under the guise of an air-conditioning device, masked tanks of lethal gas. And I was placed under standing orders to release the gas if certain circumstances should arise. Melodrama.

"The war came, of course. They worked like

demons; our medics had very little to do except circulate and snarl at sick people to lie down for a half hour if they didn't want to drop in their tracks. Our supplies chief broke down from frustration when supplies became a trickle, an erratic one. Our sponsors in the Defense Department could hardly tell a desperate major general whose division was headed for Recife without anti-tank guns that rail space was needed for something nebulous but infinitely more important. Or the President of Mexico that his capital city could not be defended because fuel was needed for something bigger than interceptor rockets. Or the Navy that a carrier launching must be postponed two months because control-system components had to be shoveled down a hole in Prospect Hill.

"Many, many times our trucks went to the appointed places at the appointed times and found only half a dozen crates in the freight car—or no freight car at all. Thank God the bombs came through. AEC must have interlocked with our operation somehow; they never shorted us, ever.

"We had a polio epidemic last year, Justin! And no vaccine! It swept through our electronics department like a prairie fire. We lost a dozen of our best men. Scores of them were crippled to the point where they could work only at benches, assembling. Only three men who really knew what they were doing were left to climb around the girders installing and testing. Volunteers made a lot of mistakes which the specialists had to undo. But things were drawing to a close. Our pilot and bombardier arrived and trained on the controls. They were good boys, just right for the job.

"It's an awesome thing, Justin. That roof up there—it's skillfully undermined. Push the button and it blasts away the crest of the hill and we stand open to the sky. One bright young man does the right things with the controls and the satellite soars and circles. The other young man does the right things with *his* controls and she spits invisible hydrogen bombs one thousand miles straight down. That was to end the war, Justin. Thirty-six hell bombs. And to keep it ended, to prove to the enemy the final insanity of continuing, there are the two specials. They've got cobalt jackets and worse than that inside. When they go, they make radionuclides that simply will not quit. So—drop one special somewhere over Finland. It blows generating lethal radioactive dust. Southwesterly winds drift the dust across most of Russia, wiping out all plant and animal life in its path. The other cobalt job's for China, even though the dust would kill as far as California. Last-chance weapons, Justin. Almost but not quite bluffs. Break glass only in case of insane continued resistance after thirty-six H-bombs destroy thirty-six Russian and Chinese population centers.

"Very close, Justin. Very close. A few hundred man-hours of electronics installation remaining, a few hundred components to procure. But then there was the surrender broadcast and my orders were clear. *This* was what the spies in the operation had been waiting for. Come hell or high water they'd get out and turn us in. My orders were—one—to release the gas in case of military defeat and capitulation. And—two—to contact responsible parties, assuming leadership of a project to complete and launch the satellite.

"I carried out the first half, Justin. You'll help me, won't you? They really can't expect a person who's been through so much to keep on going, can they? Is it reasonable? Is it fair?" His eyes were leaking again.

"If you only knew," he groaned, surrounded by his five thousand dead, immured in his guilt.

"We've got to get out of here," Justin said quietly. "We've got a long walk. Those cows'll be bellowing to be milked. Somebody might notice."

A last look at the towering satellite and they started home to milk the cows.

BOOK 2

CHAPTER ELEVEN

The shelves at Croley's store were filling up. Farm supplies were coming back. For the first time in three years neat tubes of aureomycin ointment for udder sores were neatly stacked in the old space on the shelf. Under the familiar red trademark was something new in small type about the State Antibiotics Trust. That was perfectly all right with Justin; they could call it anything they wanted as long as they were pitching in to keep his milk production up.

And then he sneered at himself for the thought. It was exactly the thought they wanted him to have, and they wanted him to chop it off right there. Not to go on and reflect: milk production for whom, where?

Half a dozen farmers were waiting for Croley. The old man came out of his miniature office, looked blankly at them, and went back in again. They sighed, studied the salt pork in his meat case, the sacks of rice from Louisiana—back after two years—and the comic books. *Billy Spencer, Northeast Farmboy. True Life Heroes*, the *Story of Klaus Fuchs*. Justin flipped through them, waiting. Billy Spencer was a clean-cut kid who lived only to make his milk norm and thereby build peace and the North American People's Democratic Republic. Disaster threatened when his butterfat production slumped 50 per cent and all the other kids jeered at him. But one night he saw a sinister figure skulking around his barn and who should it be but Benny Repler, the loudest of the jeerers. Benny, caught in the act of administering an unspecified slow poison to Billy's cows, broke down and confessed he was a tool of unreconstructed capitalist traitor saboteurs, and was marched off, head high, to expiate his sins by hard labor for the N.A.P.D.R. Billy, in a final blazing double spread, was awarded a Hero of Agricultural Labor medal by the President himself, and took the occasion to emit a hundred-word dialogue balloon pledging himself anew to the cause of peace and the people's democracy under its great protector the Soviet Union.

And as for Fuchs, the saintly worker scientist in his long martyrdom at Wormwood Scrubbs Prison—Justin carefully closed the comic book and replaced it in its wire rack.

Croley had emerged from his office again with a wrapped parcel. You could tell from the size and the neck that it was a quart bottle. "One of you call Perce," he said to the farmers. His half-witted helper was lounging in the sun on the bench outside. Justin was nearest the door. "Mr. Croley wants you," he told the boy.

The storekeeper handed Perce the wrapped bottle and told him: "Like yesterday. For the soldiers at the truck station."

Perce giggled shyly: "Soup for lunch. Like yesterday." He glanced at the farmers to see that they got his joke. They were as stone-faced as Croley and he went on his way. Croley stared sullenly at the first man in line—his way of asking: "May I help you, sir?" A haggle began about tobacco. Croley was an industrialist now; he had started a small sweatshop business in Norton. Somehow he had located a bale of prewar king-sized cigarette papers; the widows and orphans of Norton worked at home turning them into Russian-style cigarettes with cardboard mouthpieces at a cent a dozen. With dependency allotments from the Army discontinued, it fended off starvation.

"Last batch stunk," Croley said flatly. "Dime a pound and that's that. Should be glad to make a payment on your bill, Hunzicker."

Dirty pool! Hunzicker looked half around, shame on his face; everybody studiously avoided his eye. Justin wished the conventional wish that he could sink into the earth rather than see Hunzicker's shame and

Croley's gloomy arrogance.

"Right," the farmer muttered. "Dime a pound. But it's better than last time. You'll see." Croley stared, impassive. He sold the cigarettes to the garrison at Chiunga Center. The 449th Soviet Military Government Unit winked at such rampant capitalism when it was practiced by handy, steady, centrally located Mr. Croley.

Bomb him, Justin thought vacantly. Bombardment satellite's ready and waiting, short a few hundred man-hours and a crew. Find yourself the engineers and the crewmen, send 'em up, and then they drop an H-bomb on Mr. Croley and all's well.

Thirty-six lousy bombs and two specials.

He remembered a story by H. G. Wells in which the world had been threatened by nothing worse than intelligent, three-inch ants. A gunboat captain—what else could he do?—fired the big gun at the ants and steamed away knowing that he had accomplished nothing and furthermore would catch hell for shooting off the expensive ammunition.

Let's see, then. One H-bomb for Croley left thirty-five. One H-bomb for the 449th SMGU left thirty-four. If they weren't skipping numbers, that left at least 448 SMGUs to be H-bombed, leaving a deficit of 414 bombs if you didn't count the cobalt-jacketed specials, and what were they good for?

Well, you could wipe out Russia and China, including the slave laborers who used to be the North American Armies. This would leave the occupying troops here cut off from their home bases but still top dogs with their weapons, armor, and aviation. There was no reason to believe that their political bosses at home did not exert a moderating influence on the military commanders here.

And of course you couldn't even find anybody who could locate the electronics men and crewmen you needed to fire the big gun at the ants. Rawson? A hard-boiled ex-sergeant, ex-hobo, probably ex-petty criminal, somehow involved in a bomb-smuggling ring of unknown potentialities. He had not dared tell Rawson; the thing was too big for the legless man, too big for anybody who thought only in rough-and-ready action terms.

The battered, unpainted Keoka bus stopped outside the store with a scream of brakes and sizzling radiator. Justin glanced at the schedule and the clock. It was thirty-five minutes late—about average for the service.

He recognized the man who swung down from the bus and came in. The salesman. The bomb runner. *Bee-Jay Farm Supplies and Machinery, Washington, Penna.* The man pleasantly elbowed his way through the crowd, explaining to one and all: "I don't want to break in on the line, gentlemen, but you'll thank me for it in the long run. The driver tells me—How are you Mr. Croley?—the driver says we're stopping for ten minutes to let the engine cool down so I thought I'd let Mr. C. in on the big news. Gentlemen, we have milk cans again, ready for delivery, and I'm sure you're all glad to hear it. Mr. Croley, would you be interested in six dozen hundred-pound tin-lined steel milk cans of the famous Bee-Jay quality for your customers?" He had his order book out.

"C'm into the office," Croley grunted, and they disappeared.

"Things are picking up all over," a little old man said hopefully to Justin. "If the price's right, I could use a dozen myself. Sick of scouring and patching the old cans. Don't you think things are picking up?"

Somebody else snapped: "For Croley they are. Crooked skunk." The little man looked alarmed and started to move away. The dangerous talker—Justin thought he was one of the Eldridge brothers from Four Corners—took the little man's arm and began pouring into his ears a tale of how Croley paid off every week to a SMGU major who pretended to inspect his freezer room—

"Mebbe, mebbe," the little man kept saying as he tried to get away.

Justin told himself: *There's my man.* In Croley's office. I wait for him to come out, I walk along as he heads for the bus, we whisper an appointment, and I meet him somewhere. And then, thank God, it'll be over. No more bombardment satellite for me. A smooth conspiratorial group somewhere will take it over, do what has to be done. I'll have done my share. I'll watch and secretly know that someday I'll be in the history books as the daring civilian who contacted the organization at the risk of his life . . .

It didn't work out that way at all.

The bus driver called: " 'Board!" and the

salesman appeared at the door of the little office, still talking to Croley and shaking hands. He talked Croley out through the door of the shop with him, swung up the steps of the bus still talking, and collapsed comfortably into a dirty oilcloth-covered seat while Justin gaped and the bus chugged off down the road.

Contact broken.

Justin found himself swearing, almost frenzied, as he stumped along the dirt track to the Shiptons' woodlot. The flies were bad in the summer heat; he slapped viciously at them, missing oftener than not, knowing that frustration was making him behave like an idiot. *But he had to dump his load!*

Rawson came into sight about where they told him he'd be. The crippled veteran was strapped into his gocart, leaning far out to bore a hole with a post auger. The Shipton milk quota had been stepped up again. To meet it they'd have to breed their heifers early; to feed the calves that would come they needed more pasture. So here was Rawson boring postholes to enclose land supposed to be set aside as woodlot for the future.

Justin hailed the legless man abruptly. Rawson gave the pipe handle of the auger a final turn and hauled it up, loaded with sandy clay, his huge shoulder muscles bulging. "Good day's work," he said proudly. "What brings you here, Billy?"

"I know where the ghost satellite is," Justin said flatly.

Rawson grinned. "Why, so do I. Poor old

Yankee Doodle's a few miles south of Los Alamos, New Mexico, what's left of her. Too bad they didn't get her up in time—"

"I mean the real one," Justin said. "*Yankee Doodle* was deception. I know where the real one is. Rawson, you've got to put me in touch with your higher-ups. Don't act dumb, Rawson! You've got something to do with the suitcase A-bombs. I saw that salesman who picked up the assembly from me that time. He was in Croley's store but he was gone before I had a chance to talk to him."

"Near by?" Rawson asked thoughtfully.

"Skip that. Just let me know who's your boss and how to get in touch. I want to dump this business. I don't know what to do with it, where to begin. I've got to turn it over to somebody."

"You're nuts," Rawson said. "I don't know about any A-bombs and you don't know about any bombardment satellites lying around. What A-bomb was this—that liquor you helped me out with?"

"Liquor be damned! Who's your boss?"

"Convince me, Billy. You haven't yet. And if it'll help you talk, you might as well know I used to be, in my time, the youngest general officer in the Corps of Engineers."

"You're in command?"

"Of what? I'm not giving information, Billy. I'm only taking today."

So, Justin thought bitterly, I don't get to lay it down. Instead I get involved deeper. Now I have the burden of Rawson's identity on me—unless he's lying or crazy. He began to talk.

Gribble, the psychosis, the satellite.

When there was no more to tell, the legless man said: "Very circumstantial. Maybe even true."

"You'll take it from here?" Justin demanded.

"Go home and wait, Billy. Just go home and wait." Rawson shoved his gocart five feet farther down the line and stabbed his auger into the sod for the next posthole.

Justin started down the dirt path, the burden still on his back. He thought of blood-spattered cellar walls against which men exactly like him, but with less than a millionth of the guilty knowledge he possessed, were beaten and killed. When would they let Billy Justin be Billy Justin again? It went far back into childhood, his involvement. Were the old wars like this rolling, continuous thing of which he had been a part for as long as he could remember, this thing that would not end even now that it was ended? Item: childhood games. Item: high school R.O.T.C. Item: propaganda poster contests. Item: Korea (and an infected leg wound from a dirty, nameless little patrol). Item: War Three (and cows). Item: defeat and occupation. And still he was entangled in spite of his fatigue, his hundred-times-earned honorable discharge.

CHAPTER TWELVE

Justin waited through two weeks of summer drought and flies, having a minimum of talk with Gribble, collapsing every night in exhaustion. They came very close to meeting their milk norm.

The signal was a long blast of the mailwoman's horn—it meant registered mail, an insured package or something of the sort. Justin climbed the steep, short hill to the mailbox suspecting nothing more. But Betsy Cardew told him: "Think up a good reason. You're going into Chiunga Center with me."

"Rawson?" he asked. She nodded. "Can you wait while I throw a bucket of water over myself and change my shirt?"

"I can't. Please get in."

They chugged the long mail route almost without conversation. She had nothing to say except that he would meet some people. He tried to tell her that she shouldn't be mixed up in anything like this and she said she had to be. They had to have the mail carriers. And, after reflecting, he realized that they did. Mail carriers were daily travelers who met everybody and carried packages as part of the job. Mail carriers were essential, and if one of them happened to be a slim, clear-eyed girl entirely unsuited for torture and death in a cellar, so much the worse for her.

She showed no fear at the check points. The Red Army men who stopped her and signed her through on the registers were friendly. She said to them, *"Prohsteetye, chtoh behspohkohyoo vas,"* while Justin stared and the soldiers grinned.

"Very difficult language," she told Justin as they drove on. "I'm making slow progress."

"Those soldiers looked pretty sloppy to me."

"Colonel Platov got a girl. Mrs. Grauer."

Justin whistled. The Grauers were Chiunga Center aristocracy. Young Mr. Grauer was president by primogeniture of the feed mill, Mrs. Grauer was an imported Wellesley girl and very slim and lovely. The husband, of course, was whereabouts-unknown after surrendering his National Guard regiment in the debacle at El Paso. "He goes right to the house?" he asked.

"Right to the big red brick Georgian show place," she said, concentrating on her driving.

"I don't know if they're in love or not. There's an awful lot of it going on."

So Colonel Platov had a girl and the soldiers at the check points had murky brass and had skipped shaving. The soldierly virtue was running fast out of SMGU 449. Justin was suddenly more conscious than ever that he smelled like what he was: a farmer in a midsummer drought.

Justin got out when they reached the post office by late afternoon. Betsy Cardew said she had two hours of sorting ahead of her, and would he meet her at her house on Chiunga Hill.

He wandered through the town unmolested. Mr. Farish, the bald, asthmatic young pharmacist, called to him from behind his prescription counter as he strolled down High Street. Mr. Farish and he had been fellow members of Rotary in the old days before the Farm-or-Fight Law; the membership of a freelance commercial artist made Chiunga Center Rotary more broad-minded and cultured than the other chapters down the valley. They valued him for it, especially Mr. Farish who daydreamed of escaping from pharmacy via an interminable historical novel he was writing.

Justin stepped into the store and nervously blurted out his cover story, an unconvincing bit about buying seed cake from the local feed store, Croley's price being too high for comfort.

Mr. Farish, completely uninterested, waved the yarn aside and set him up a root beer.

"Red Army boys are crazy about root beer," he said. "Nothing like it where they come from."

"How're they behaving?"

"Pretty fair. Say, did you hear about Colonel Platov and Mrs.——?"

"I heard. Customer, Fred."

It was a Red soldier with a roll of film. *"Sredah?"* he asked, grinning.

"Pyatneetsah," Mr. Farish told him. "O.K.?"

"Hokay," said the soldier. He contorted his face and brought out from the depths: "Soap?" And grinned with relief.

Mr. Farish sold him the soap and put away the film. "He wanted it on Wednesday and I told him Friday," he said casually. "You saw how he took it, Billy. There's no harm in them. Of course, you farmers are eating a lot better than we are here but after they get food distribution squared away——"

Justin gulped his root beer and thanked Farish. He had to find out about that seed cake, he said, and hurried out. The bald young man looked hurt by his abruptness.

The bald young idiot!

He headed for one of the elm-shaded residential streets and paced its length, his hands rammed into the pockets of his jeans. Farish didn't know; Farish knew only that farmers were always griping. He didn't realize that the problem facing the Reds in the valley was to squeeze the maximum amount of milk from it and any time spent batting the mercantile population around would be wasted. After the pattern was set, after the dairy farmers were automatic serfs, then they would move on the shopkeepers. Currently they were being used, and skillfully, to supply the garrison and the farms.

And still there was a nagging doubt that these Red G.I.s were just human, and that their bosses were just human, that things seemed to be easing into a friendlier pattern of live and let live.

And beneath that one there was the darker thought that it was too good to last, that somehow the gigantic self-regulating system would respond to the fact that Red G.I.s were treating the conquered population like friends and that Colonel Platov had a girl.

An off-duty soldier and *his* girl were strolling the elm-shaded street with him, he noticed. The girl he vaguely recognized: one of those town drifters who serves your coffee at the diner one morning and the next day, to your surprise, is selling you crockery at the five-and-ten. Margaret something-or-other——

A sergeant bore down on the couple, and the soldier popped to attention, saluting. Without understanding a word Justin knew that he was witnessing a memorable chewing-out. The spitting, snarling Russian language was well suited to the purpose. When it ended at last, the chastened soldier saluted, about-faced, and marched down the street at attention, with Margaret something-or-other left standing flat-footed. The sergeant relaxed and smiled at her: *Kahkoy, preeyatnyi syoorpreez!"*

Margaret had her bearings again. She smiled, *"Da,* big boy. Let's go," and off they went arm in arm.

Justin walked back to High Street, deeply disturbed. He liked what he had seen. It was too good, too warmly human, to be true.

Mr. Sparhawk was established on a crate at the corner of High and Onondaga outside the bank preaching to a thin crowd, none of whom stayed for more than a minute. The pinched British voice and the bony British face had not changed in the months since Justin last saw him. Neither had his line:

"My dear friends, we have peace at last. Some of you doubtless believe that it would be a better peace if it had been won by the victory of the North American Governments than by their adversaries, but this is vain thinking. Peace is indivisible, however attained. It is not what it has come out of but what we make of it. Reforming ourselves from within is the way in which we shall reform society. In the lonely individual heart begins what you are pleased to call progress. I rejoice that there is a diminished supply of meat and pray that this condition will reveal to you all the untruthfulness of the propaganda that meat is essential to health, and that from this realization many of you will progress to vegetarianism, the first great ascetic step along the road to universal life-reverence . . ."

Justin could not stand more than a minute of it himself. He headed north along Onondaga Street toward Chiunga Hill and the big white house where Betsy lived. He knew why it hadn't been requisitioned, even after the guilty flight of her father, the National Committeeman. The Russians were supposed to live like Spartans in their barracks, officers faring not much better than the troops. But he thought he scented a trend in town that would end only with the expropriation of every decent dwelling in the Center.

The second and third floors of the house were closed off. There was still plenty of room for Betsy and a Mrs. Norse, the last of the servants. She was tottery and deaf; actually the two women waited on each other. Betsy matter-of-factly offered Justin a bath, which he eagerly accepted. When he emerged from the tub, she called to him: "I've found some of my father's gardening things for you to put on. I don't suppose you want me to save your clothes?"

"No," he called back, embarrassed. "You caught me by surprise today, you know. I was wearing them just to clean the barn——"

"Of course," she said politely. "I'll have Mrs. Norse burn them, shall I?"

Clean socks, underwear, and clean, faded denims—he had to take up six inches of slack with his belt—left Justin feeling better than he had in months. Mrs. Norse was noisy about the improvement. She remembered the day when a man wouldn't dream of setting foot outside his bedroom unless he was decently clothed in stiff collar, white shirt, tie, and jacket. She told Justin about it and Betsy cooked dinner.

A panel truck pulled into the driveway while they were eating spanish rice, the main dish. It proceeded on to the back of the house, but Justin had time to read the lettering on it as it passed the window.

" 'Department of Agriculture,' " he said to Betsy. "And in smaller letters, 'Fish and Wild Life Survey.' "

She was blank-faced. "Go into the library when you've finished," she said. "Mrs. Norse and I will clear things up." He found he was gobbling his spanish rice and deliberately slowed down. Then the stuff balled in his mouth so he couldn't swallow.

There were three men, all strangers, all middle-aged. One was the lean little gnome type, one was heavy and spectacularly bald, one was a placid ox.

Mr. Ox said, "Put up your hands," and searched him. Mr. Egg said, "I hope you don't mind. We have to ask you some questions," and Justin knew at once who he was—The Honorable James Buchanan Wagner, junior senator from Michigan, nicknamed "Curly." He had shaved his head, and for safety's sake really ought to do something about his superb voice. Though perhaps, Justin thought, he as a commercial artist was a lot quicker than most to fill in the outlines of that bushy head.

Mr. Gnome said, "Sit down, please," and opened a brief case. He laid a light tray and variously colored tiles before Justin and said: "Put them in the tray any way you like." Justin built up a nice design for the man in about a minute and sat back.

Mr. Gnome said: "Look at this picture and tell me what it's about." The picture was very confusing, but after a moment Justin realized that it was a drawing of one man telling another man something, apparently a secret from their furtive expressions. He said so.

"Now what about this one?"

"Two men fighting. The big one's losing the fight."

"This one?"

"A horse—just a horse."

There were about fifty pictures. When they were run through, Mr. Gnome switched to ink-blot cards, which Justin identified as spiders, women, mirrors, and whatever else they looked like to him.

Every now and then Justin heard Senator Wagner distinctly mutter, "Fiddle-faddle," which did not surprise him. The senator, known as a man who saw his duty to the United States and did it, was nevertheless not distinguished for broad-gauged, liberal leadership.

There followed word-association lists. Not only did the gnome hold a stop watch, but Mr. Ox calmly donned a stethoscope and put the button on Justin's wrist.

Then they seemed to be finished. The gnome told the senator: "I guess he's all right. Yes—he's either smarter than I am or he's all right. Sincere, not too neurotic, a reasonably effective person. For what it's worth, Senator, I vouch for——"

The senator said angrily: "No names!"

Mr. Gnome shrugged. "His reaction time on 'Congress,' 'hair,' 'wagon'—he recognized you all right."

"Very well, Doctor," rumbled the celebrated voice. "Mr. Justin, I wish to show you something." The senator turned down his collar on the right. He was still bitterly hostile—fundamentally scared, Justin realized, with two kinds of fear. There was the built-in animal fear of pain, mutilation, death. There was the abstract fear that one wrong decision at any stage of this dangerous game would blow sky-high any hope that America would rise again.

The senator was showing Justin a razor blade taped inside his collar. "You can seem merely to be easing your collar, Mr. Justin. With one swift move, however—*so*—you can slash your cartoid artery beyond repair. Within seconds you will be dead. Your orders are not to be taken alive," the senator said. And he added grimly: "My psychologist friend indicates that you have sufficient moral fiber to carry them out." He tossed a blade and an inch of tape at Justin. "Put them on. Then tell your story. General Hollerith assures us through Miss Cardew that it is of the utmost importance."

"Is Hollerith Rawson?" Justin demanded.

"I don't recall his cover name. No legs," said the psychologist.

His friend Rawson a general after all. Then what might not be true? The psychologist slipped out while Justin told Senator Wagner and Mr. Ox—of the FBI?—about his bombardment satellite.

The senator was apoplectic. He fizzed for minutes about abuse of the executive power; apparently Congress had been told as little about the bombardment satellite as an earlier Congress had been told about the atomic bomb. Well—sigh—what's done is done. Now the problem is to integrate the windfall into existing plans.

Mr. Gnome returned and said: "Miss Cardew will brief you, Mr. Justin. We have to be on our way now."

They left and Justin heard the Fish and Wild Life Survey panel truck move out of the driveway and down the road.

Back in the dining room Miss Norse was dozing in a corner.

"Well?" asked Betsy Cardew.

He turned down his collar and showed her the blade.

"The man said you were in and I was to brief you. What do you want to know about us?"

"What's there to know? How many. What you plan. Whether you think you can get away with it. Who's the boss?"

"I don't know how many there are. I don't really *know* whether there's anybody in it except a couple of local people and those three. They came around a month ago—I used to know the senator. I don't know who's in charge, if anybody.

"They told me it's a war plan, one of those things that lies in the files until it's needed. Well, it was needed when the collapse came at

El Paso. The orders were for as many atomic-service officers as possible to grab all the fissionable material they could lay their hands on and go underground. The same for psychological-warfare personnel. Then start recruiting civilians into the organization."

"And what do we *do?*"

"They've mentioned a winter uprising. They hope by then to have a large part of the civilian population alerted. There should be food caches, caches of winter clothing, weapons, and ammunition stolen from Red supply dumps. Then you wait for real socked-in, no-see flying weather and fire your suitcase A-bombs. Washington, of course, to behead the Administration. Ports to prevent reinforcement. Tank parks. Roads and railways. Simultaneously a scorched-earth guerrilla war against the garrisons while they're cut off.

"Oh, and you asked me whether I think we can get away with it, didn't you? The answer is no. I don't think so. I don't see anything coming out of it except defeat and retaliation. But is there anything else to do?"

"No," he said gravely. Nor was there.

"What did you tell General Hollerith, anyway?" she asked. "Something to do with Gribble, wasn't it?"

"Sorry. They asked me not to say." He fished for a change of subject. "How did you arrange the meeting, get in touch with them? If it's all right for me to know."

"I suppose so. Believe it or not, our conspiracy has a complete secret telegraphic network covering most of the United States. *I* didn't believe them when they told me, but it's true. Like finding out that you don't have to dig a tunnel under the English Channel; there's one already dug. The senator found out about the wires when he was on the crime commission. They call them 'dry wires.' They're the old Postal Telegraph network from before your time and mine. Public clocks in all sorts of places used to get correcting pulses over the wires. When Western Union absorbed Postal Telegraph, they just blanked off their clock wires because radio had come along by then and any disc jockey could give you Naval Observatory time. I located one of the painted-over terminals in the Lackawanna station. Ticket clerk there's in with us. All you need to activate a link of the circuit are a battery, a key, and a buzzer. He covers the wire for us. A brave man, Billy . . ."

"We're all heroes," he said bitterly.

"Yes, I suppose we are. Would you like a drink?"

"I ought to start for home. Maybe I can hitch a ride."

"Nonsense. Stay the night and take the Keoka bus. If you stay for breakfast it'll improve your cover story. I think I told you—there's a lot of it going on."

"I think what you said was, 'It isn't love, but there a lot of it going on'."

"Something like that. There isn't much love around these days. A lot of loneliness, a lot of monotony, a lot of shattered pride."

"I'll take that drink, please," he said.

CHAPTER THIRTEEN

They walked together down Chiunga Hill toward the town, savoring the still cool morning. The reservoir off to the north was a sheet of blue grass and the pumping station a toy fort in the clear air.

"I'm glad they never bombed us," Betsy said. "I really like this place."

He thought of reminding her what a scorched-earth guerrilla campaign meant, but did not speak.

"Convoy," Betsy said, pointing down at the highway. The buglike trucks must be hauling supplies—but the tanks? "Maneuvers somewhere," she said.

They walked on in silence, and Chiunga Hill Road became Elm Street and they joined

other morning walkers to work. A letter
carrier in gray said: "Morning, Miss Cardew.
What do you suppose those trucks are up to?"

He meant the convoy. Instead of by-passing
the town they had turned off the highway and
were rolling down High Street, three blocks
farther on.

"Maybe they're going across the bridge to
the Tunkhannock road, Mr. Selwin. Mr.
Selwin, do you know Mr. Justin?"

"I don't believe I've had the pleasure," the
old man said. "You a farmer, Mr. Justin."

"Yes."

"You're a lucky man, then, I can tell you
that. At least you get all you want to eat. Say,
Mr. Justin, I hear that sometimes you people
up in the hills have a few eggs or maybe a
chicken or some butter left over and I happen
to know a family with a little girl that's real
sick with anemia. Blood needs building up.
Now if I could fix it up with you——"

Justin shook his head. "I can't get away
with it, Mr. Selwin. I'm very sorry. And by the
way, the farmers may be eating better than
the city people, but they're sweating it right
out again making milk. The norm's always
moving up, you know. Soon as you catch up, it
jumps again."

"He's telling the truth, Mr. Selwin," Betsy
said. "Ask any of the rural carriers. Surely
those trucks aren't stopping for our little
traffic light, are they?"

"They never have before," Mr. Selwin said.
They were now only a block from High Street.
The postman peered over his glasses at the

standing trucks. "But then," he said, "they don't seem to be regular Red Army trucks. Instead of the red star they have—let's see—MBA. What's MBA mean?"

"In the first place," Betsy said slowly, "it's MVD."

"Beats me, Miss Cardew. I don't know how you and the other young people do it." He winked at Justin privately.

"They're the border guards. And the political police," Betsy said.

Two trucks turned out of line on High Street and came roaring down their way along Elm. Justin got only a glimpse of young faces and special uniforms. Green, with polished leather.

They can't have come for us, thought Justin incredulously. There's a *regiment* of them. Fifty personnel-carrier trucks, command cars, half a dozen medium tanks. They can't have come for Betsy and me!

Walking in frozen silence, they reached High Street. The main body of the convoy was parked there, the young men in their special uniforms impassive under the eyes and whispers of five hundred work-bound men and women. At the far end of High Street, on the old bridge across the Susquehanna, stood two of the tanks. The four other tanks were crawling northeast from High along Seneca. Nothing was in that direction except the high school—the 449th SMGU garrison.

A fat man in a high-slung command car got up, looked at his watch, and blew a whistle three times. The convoy erupted into action.

People laughed shrilly; it was comical to see almost one thousand young men who had been stock-still a moment ago begin to climb out of their trucks, hand down equipment, consult maps and lists, snap salutes, and pass low-toned commands and acknowledgements.

A pattern appeared. Justin knew it from Korea. There are only so many ways to occupy a town. This outfit was doing it in the expensive, foolproof sledge-hammer way. The strings of sixteen burdened men in double column were machine-gun sections streaming out to the perimeter of the area; they would set up a pair of cross-firing guns at each main road into the Center. The squads double-timing ahead of them would be pickets linking the machine-gun points. And there was a mortar section, sagging under their bedplates and barrels and canvas vests stuffed with bombs; they were on their way to the Susquehanna bridge embankment to reinforce the pair of tanks. A cheap little mortar bomb would sink a rowboat unworthy of a 155-millimeter shell from the tank; a white phosphorous bomb would be more effective against forbidden swimmers than machine-gun fire.

And the specialist squads moved down to the railroad station to hold all trains, and into the small A.T. & T. building to take charge of communications, and into the Western Union office with its yellow and black hanging sign and varnished golden-oak counter and scared nineteen-year-old girl clerk.

And riflemen consulted maps and went and stood like traffic cops, a pair at every intersection, sweeping the crowded sidewalks with stony eyes.

Beside Justin, Mr. Selwin gibbered: "It must be some kind of drill, don't you think? Just what you call a dry run, don't it look like?"

A vast relief was blossoming inside Justin. "I think so," he said. "I can't imagine what else it could be. Just practice in case." *In case of me—but not yet.*

A sound truck rolled down the streets, stopping at each corner to make an announcement in Russian and one in English. They saw the crowds melt from the sidewalk and into shops as it approached; from three blocks away they caught the English: "All persons off the streets at once and await further inspections. Persons on the streets in three minutes will be shot——"

They dived for a store the instant it sank in. The store happened to be Mr. Farish's pharmacy. "Thank God," said Betsy. "A place with coffee." Her voice shook.

The sound truck stopped only a couple of yards away at the intersection and bellowed in Russian and English. The score or so of people crowded into the store debated on the Russian announcement. They more or less agreed at last that the announcement had been orders for all SMGU troops to report at once to the high school athletic field.

Bald young Mr. Farish was behind his soda fountain making and serving coffee mechanically. When he got to Justin, Betsy, and Mr. Selwin, he twinkled: "Little break in the monotony, eh?"

Mr. Selwin said: "I ought to be in the sorting room. I've been late before this year, no fault of my own. It's going to look awfully bad."

The coffee was some terrible synthetic or other.

Betsy said from the window: "They're arresting the SMGU men—I think." Everybody crowded up to see a couple of regular-detachment people being marched along by MVD troops. The green-uniformed young men had taken the regulars' tommy guns.

"It's something like a visit from the inspector general," said a man who actually took a short step through the door onto the sidewalk to see better. "Only—Russian." One of the MVD men posted like traffic cops yelled at him and brandished his rifle. He grinned and ducked back into the store.

"Russians don't scare me any more," he announced. "You know what I mean. I thought it was the end of the world when they came, but I learned. They're G.I.s, and so what?"

A woman looked around, scowled, and said: "Speak for yourself."

It precipitated a ten-minute debate in the crowded little store. Chiunga Center had not yet decided on the relationship between itself and the Russians. "We might be across the Mississippi," said somebody. "How'd you like to have a bunch of Chinks swaggering around? Yeah, the Russians aren't so different from Americans. It says in the *Times* they both have characters shaped by frontiers . . ." A Toynbeean's view was that the occupiers would be softened and democratized by their contact with the occupied.

Through it all Justin and Betsy stood in a rear corner, their hands nervously entwined. Mr. Selwin left them long enough for a worried glance through the window. While the old man was gone, Justin had time to mutter. "Have you got a blade? I could buy one for you."

"I have one," she said, barely moving her lips.

Mr. Selwin came back. "I believe it's all over," he said. "The streets are clear and those soldiers are just standing there and I ought to get to the sorting room."

"Better not, Mr. Selwin," Betsy said.

"You don't understand, Miss Cardew. You just took a mail job because you had to work at something. I've got thirty-two years in and absences don't look good when a man's my age. They start to say you're slipping. Young people don't understand that. I believe I'm going to ask that soldier if I can go now."

"I wouldn't, Mr. Selwin," Justin told him.

Selwin went anyway. He shouted from the doorway at the pair of riflemen: "Is it all right now? We go? Free?" They stared at him.

Some of the other Americans stranded in the store called out hopefully in Russian. The faces of the young men in green didn't change. "Better not," a man told Mr. Selwin.

Mr. Selwin said: "I'll try a few steps out. It all seems to be over anyway."

He stepped out tentatively, keeping his eye on the Russians. They simply watched incuriously. The postman turned and grinned for a moment at the people in the store and took a couple of cautious steps down the street, then a couple more.

One of the Russians raised his rifle and shot Mr. Selwin in the chest. The big bullet blasted a grunt out of the old man, but after he fell he was silent. Apparently the sentry had been waiting for Mr. Selwin to step past the glass window of the drugstore to brick wall that would provide a backstop.

The man who wasn't scared any more said slowly: "I think this is a different kind of Russian we have here."

A middle-aged woman began to whoop and sob with hysteria. Mr. Farish yelled: "Don't let her knock those bottles over, please! I'll get some ammonia spirits——"

He fed them to her from a glass, nervously stroking his bald head. She calmed down, took the glass in her own hands and gulped, coughing.

They heard the boom of the sound truck in the distance again, and another sound: machine guns, a pair of them firing short, carefully spaced bursts. "It isn't combat firing," Justin said in bewilderment. "It sounds as if they're shooting for badges on a range."

Then a spattering of rifle shots confused the sound and then the truck rolled down High Street and drowned out the small arms with its yammer.

"All persons registered with the 449th

Soviet Military Government Unit are ordered
to report at once to the athletic field.
Stragglers will be fired on. All persons
registered . . ."

After the case of Mr. Selwin they did not
hesitate. The shops along High Street erupted
civilians who streamed toward the field, some
of them running.

The field was clear on the other side of town
from High Street. The congestion as they
neared it was worse than it had ever been for
a Saturday football game, even the traditional
rivalry of Chiunga Catamounts versus Keoka
Cougars. The bellowing sound truck dimmed
behind them. The queer and prissy bursts-of-
four machine gunning became louder, with
the occasional spatter of rifles still occurring
now and then.

Green-uniformed MVD men were posted
around the field, gesturing the crowd
through. One man was going the wrong way;
he charged out of the gate beneath the stands,
stumbling and caroming off the incoming
civilians. Justin dodged and yanked Betsy
aside as the man leaned over and was sick.
Then the crowd swept them on through the
narrow gate. They popped out inside on the
cinder track that circled the field; MVD men
gestured them along. The small bleachers
across the field from them and the small
stands sloping back behind them were full;
these late arrivals were to be standees.

The field itself was crowded with
something Justin at first—idiotically—took
to be a dress parade. As he and Betsy shuffled

sideways along the cinder track under the pressure of more arrivals, his eyes gradually sorted out the two thousand odd soldiers on the field.

First there were the disarmed men of the 449th rigidly at attention behind their officers. They were drawn up in a solid block of companies that stretched from the north goal line to the 30-yard line. Everybody was there, down to the medics in their hospital coats and the cooks and bakers in their whites.

Then he saw the tanks, one at each corner of the field, their machine guns and cannon depressed to fire point-blank into the 449th. Then he saw the green-uniformed MVD men with rifles and tommy guns and a pile of new dead directly before them on the 50-yard line.

Machine guns roared above his head. Betsy screamed and clapped her hands to her head. The muzzle blast was terrific——

He turned and saw where they were coming from. A pair of them was mounted in the little press box hung from the roof of the stands, the box where the *Valley News* used to cover the games and WVC-TV used to broadcast the traditional rivalry each year. The guns hammered with that firing-range artificiality for a while and then stopped. Justin noticed that directly in front of them in midfield five soldiers of the 449th lay butchered.

Somebody in the field bawled: *"Roh-tah—gay!"*

MVD men began to hustle officers and men from one of the company blocks. All the officers, one enlisted man in four. The uneven rifle shots were explained while the selection was going on. One of the enlisted men broke loose and ran, screaming, when a green-uniformed youth tapped his chest. He was shot down as he sprinted sweatily toward the bleachers. The rest moved like zombies to the killing ground. In a few seconds they too were sprawling and screaming while the plunging fire from the press box hacked up the carefully tended sod of the stadium.

The word was traveling from early arrivals in the stands to those who had come late and were jammed onto the track. "They made a big speech in Russian and English first," a man next to Justin reported after whispers with *his* neighbors. He spoke to Justin, but he couldn't take his eyes off the charnel heap in the infield. His face and voice were just a little insane. "Fella says they called the 449th traitors to international socialism. Stuff about sloth, negligence, corruption, disgrace to the Army. Then they shot all the top brass, starting with Platov. Say, did you hear about Platov and Mrs.——?"

"I heard," Justin said. He turned away.

"Rohtah gay," Betsy whispered. "Company G. That's only the fourth in their alphabet. They'll be busy all morning."

They were.

At noon the last of the job was done. The weeping, or blank-faced, or madly grinning survivors of the 449th were loaded onto trucks and the field PA system cleared its throat.

"Proclamation. To the indigenous population of the area formerly under control of the 449th Soviet Military Government Unit. You are ordered to inform all persons unable to attend the foregoing demonstration of what has happened. You are advised that this is the treatment that will be accorded to such betrayers of international socialist morality as the late Platov and his gang of bourgeois-spirited lackeys. You are advised that henceforth this area will be under the direction of the *Meeneestyerstvoh Vnootrenikh Dyehl*, the Ministry of Internal Affairs. You are advised that all laws and rules of the occupation will be rigidly enforced from this moment on. You are ordered to disperse within ten minutes. Troops will fire on stragglers."

This might have been intended to precipitate a panic and an excuse for slaughter. It did not. Justin, sated with the horror of the morning's work, still had some room for pride in him when the people in the stands and bleachers rose and slowly filed from the stadium, turned their backs on the green-uniformed young monsters and their pile of carrion without cringing.

Justin walked with Betsy to the post office and left her there with a silent squeeze of the hand.

At the restaurant that doubled as bus station an old woman told him: "No busses been along all morning, mister. Should of been the Keoka bus at eight, ten, and twelve. And this fella in the green with the fancy belt, he walked in and he ripped down the bus schedule right off the wall. I guess he didn't speak English, but then I guess he didn't have to, did he?"

"I guess not," Justin said.

He went out and started the fifteen-mile walk home under the broiling midsummer sun.

BOOK 3

CHAPTER FOURTEEN

Justin was scything down the dry grass of autumn for winter feeding to the cows. Behind him Gribble followed with a rake and a hoarded ball of twine ends, making bundles they could carry to the barn.

It was October.

In the monotony of scything, the hypnotic *step—swing—slice—step—swing—slice*, Justin could almost believe in the role he was playing. Of all the roles he had played, it was the queerest. Successively he had impersonated a grownup, a soldier, a business artist, a farm front fighter. Now what he had to tell himself was: "You're a peasant. This is what it's like to be a peasant."

And he was. Dirty, coarsened, tired and

underfed, Justin, who had supposed himself a democrat all his life, found himself at last a member of the eternal overwhelming majority, brother at last in space and time to the stone-age grubbers of roots, the Chinese toiling with an aching back and thighs over rice shoots in the dynasty of Han or Comrade Mao, potato eaters of the Andes or the Netherlands, all those who in time past, time present, and perhaps for all time to come must dig in stubborn ground while the knees shake with fatigue. The emblem of the brotherhood was hunger and fatigue.

Three months under the *Meeneestyerstvoh Vnootrenikh Dyehl* had left him a clear choice. He could be a debased animal or he could die.

He knew of people by the dozen who had chosen to be people. They had died. There was the case of the Wehrweins of Straw Hill. The Wehrweins refused to understand that things were different now. They refused to make their quota, trusting to the farmer's old technique of the blank stare, the Who-me-mister? and the sullen " 'Tain't no business of mine." A polite search would have shown them nothing, but the MVD searched with crowbars and found a hoard of grain.

The Wehrweins were shot for sabotage. Their children were shot for failing to report their sabotage.

The Elekinnens of Little Finland, one of those big close-knit European family complexes, were wiped out to the last man, woman, and child. Papa Gunder, their patriarch, cursed and struck an MVD Agro section inspector: unlawful violence against the occupying authority.

Mr. Konreid made no more popskull brandy from his sprawling, slovenly vineyard. Mr. Konreid had been shot for failure to obey agricultural crop-acreage regulations. His fifty-year-old son and the son's fifty-year-old wife, workers in the feed mill, town dwellers who had not seen the old man since a bitter estrangement three decades ago, died with him in the center of the athletic field: failure to report contravention of agricultural regulations.

There was a new whispered phrase, "shipped South." Mr. and Mrs. Lacey of Four Corners had been "shipped South." They were back in two weeks, cringing away from questions, seemingly half insane. All their teeth had been pulled and they worked their fields with lunatic zeal. The four nearest neighbors of the Laceys were arrested shortly after by MVD teams who knew exactly where to find their hoards of grain, the eggs laid down in water glass, the secret smokehouse in the wood where hams and bacon slowly turned on strings over smoldering hickory chips. The neighbors were shot.

There were never audible complaints any more, through two milk-norm increases and two ration reductions. Everybody had taken to frantic weeding in every spare second; leisure did not exist. The smallest children were pressed into work. A three-year-old who carelessly tore out a turnip top instead of parasitic wild mustard was beaten and did not eat that night. Possibly a generation of permissive-discipline pediatricians were whirling in their graves, but the pediatricians had not expected that American parents, comfortable in mortgaged homes, secure in union contracts, nourished at glittering supermarkets, neat in their K-Mart dresses and no-iron suits would soon rejoin the eternal majority of hunger and fatigue.

Even the great American bathroom was a mockery. Nobody talked about it but everybody was squeezing the utmost from his land by manuring with human excrement, an Oriental practice from which the fortunate North Americans has been excused by virtue of the Haber process, Peruvian guano, and Mexican phosphate rock. But there was no fertilizer compounded of nitrates, guano, and phosphorous to be had at Croley's store these days. Presumably it was being shipped directly to Russia and China.

Justin, shorter, darker, and dirtier than he had been two months ago, stooped and swung his scythe. Gribble absolutely couldn't get the hang of it, not after days of hand-blistering practice. The co-ordination wasn't there. The little man and his shattered nervous system were good for nothing but gleaning with a sickle behind Justin, raking and bundling.

Had there once been one-man balers? Had there really? Had one man, proudly astride a snorting red tractor, chugged down a field, importantly leaning far out and peering behind him as the scoop swept up mowed windrows, the plunging tamper arm compacted the hay, the binder twirled cord around and tied, and the machine bumpingly ejected bale after perfect bale?

Justin now was a citizen of the North American People's Democratic Republic, at last in formal existence months after its currency had gone into circulation. Everybody had been ordered to report to the Center for ceremonies and a spontaneous demonstration. Betsy Cardew was prominent in the demonstration. She had joined the Party of the People and worked at it with shrill fanaticism. Condescendingly mentioned in one speech as a tireless worker for the cause of peace and democracy, she looked, when Justin met her occasionally at the mailbox, very tired indeed. She sometimes passed him a note, because now there was a tape recorder behind the dashboard of her car.

When one of the notes said something like, "Still heard nothing. Must hv been picked up. Prsme used bldes in time snce we're still at lrge. Billy, Billy, how I wish——Wht's use?" he would start to recall that he belonged to a conspiracy of the oppressed, that he was the trigger man of the bombardment satellite. And that one step outside the narrow lines would mean his death.

It was easier to go on mowing than to stop and let his muscles knot up in the first cutting winds from the north. They had to get in the hay. They had to fell trees in the woodlot and buck them up with a Swedish saw and split

them for the stove. Dry autumn was going to
be followed by cold winter. There would be no
coal or oil; fossil fuels were for Russia and
China these days.

The North American People's Democratic
Republic was born, puppet of Asia, and the
United States of America—obstinately the
consciousness of it would not die—was a
puppet's slave. Chiunga County produced a
"surplus" of food—while its inhabitants were
verging on starvation—that went to New York
for shipment to Russia in a steady flow with
shipments from thousands of other rural
counties.

But whispered tales said the factory cities
were worse! It was easy to imagine how, once
self-pity admitted the possibility. Barracks.
Two twelve-hour shifts. Starvation rations at
a patrolled mess hall. A belt line whose speed
could be pushed up imperceptibly until you
dropped at your job—and were flogged or
shot for dropping.

And whispered tales said the young men
and women of the North American armies
were toiling half at reclamation projects in
the Soviet Arctic, the rest in the arid Chinese
interior.

Of course they would never come back.

Even to the peasant that Billy Justin had
turned into the brutal audacity of the over-all
plan was slowly becoming clear. It was
attrition of the U.S. population. The oldsters
were to die off gradually of scanty food and
pneumonia—the coming winter without fuel
would sweep like his scythe through the

population. The youngsters who would normally make up the loss were safely in the Arctic and the Gobi.

Within a couple of years more Russians and Chinese would begin to arrive—colonists this time instead of soldiers.

The senator, the psychologist, and the FBI man were dust by now.

The Postal Telegraph "dry wire," still guarded at fantastic risk by the ticket seller in the railroad station, was silent and had been for two months.

Rawson—but he was a general named Hollerith, wasn't he?—could only say he knew nothing, he had heard nothing, they must wait.

Betsy Cardew was dying by inches of fatigue and strain, impersonating a fanatical convert, waiting for the hand on her shoulder, praying there would be time for her to first open her cartoid artery.

There was nothing he could do. There was absolutely nothing he could do. All he could do was scythe down the dry grass, stop every dozen paces, and sweep the whetstone twice along the worn steel blade. It was important to keep the blade keen; a dull scythe crushed down the grass instead of slicing it. Grass crushed to the ground was wasted and he would need every blade of it to see the small herd through the winter.

He woke from his daze to find himself at the end of the field of redtop. Beyond was the stubble of his corn land, which had been reaped for silage a month ago. He looked around and saw Gribble far behind him, doggedly raking. And behind Gribble an approaching figure, tall and gaunt as a scarecrow.

"Hello there, William," called Mr. Sparhawk. "I've come for a bit of dinner and a pallet for the night. Don't mind, old boy, do you?"

CHAPTER FIFTEEN

It was the hour after dinner. These days that meant the hour when quarrels flared between Justin and the feeble, whining Gribble. There was something about a meal utterly without pleasure that your temper couldn't take. No coffee, not even synthetic, no pepper or spices, no dessert, no meat. They dined on baked mashed potatoes with an unsuccessful experiment at cheesemaking sprinkled over the top. Boiled greens on the side. They lay like stones in the stomach.

It was the hour for Justin to curse Gribble for his laziness and Gribble to cower and complain.

Mr. Sparhawk was there that night, however. He had said a heathen grace, eaten sparingly of the potatoes—apologetically scraping off the unsuccessful cheese topping—and finally excused himself to sit on the floor cross-legged. He looked about the same as ever. His rucksack was worn, he had a new peeled branch for a staff, and he wore jeans instead of Red Army pants and shirt. He talked less than usual, perhaps judging that Justin would welcome an excuse to throw him out.

Justin studied the old man morosely. There was something awfully peculiar about his presence, something he couldn't put his finger on.

"Where've you been lately?" he asked.

"South to Maryland. North to Vermont. Where the Ground that is the Oversoul bade me——"

"I didn't ask you that, damn you!"

Mr. Sparhawk shrugged apologetically, but he couldn't resist preaching. "I forgive your curse," he said. "I know that in your present incarnation you're still Earth-and-Appetite-bound——"

"Maryland and Vermont." Justin slowly ruminated. "How?"

Mr. Sparhawk looked politely baffled. "I'm sorry, William," he said. "Your question conveys nothing to me."

"I mean *how?* How do you travel? How do you get through the check points? Why aren't you picked up?"

"Oh," Mr. Sparhawk said, surprised. "But I am. Often."

"And what *happens?*"

Modesty and pride struggled visibly on the old man's face. At last he said: "When it's a case of the other ranks—privates and noncoms—you'd say—I reluctantly put on an outworn garment." He stood to attention and his mild face hardened. The jaw thrust out and the very nose seemed to turn into a predator's beak. "Damn you," Sparhawk rasped, "what's the meaning of this? How dare you obstruct a loyal citizen and a minister of the gospel? By God, you popinjays stand aside or your superiors shall hear of it and so much the worse for you!"

The windowpanes rattled. Justin and Gribble quailed before his raucous, righteous anger and authority. Mr. Sparhawk smiled apologetically and folded into a cross-legged squat again. "It usually works," he said mildly. "When it doesn't, I'm brought in for questioning. Officers tend to bring one in no matter what one does, so when confronted with a commission I spare myself the necessity of reverting to my evil old ways.

"Once I'm in the local chokey I politely but firmly invoke the North American People's Democratic Republic guarantee of freedom of worship, I explain politely, is to wander and preach. To make a long story short, William, I'm usually released after a couple of days, though once I was held as long as a week. Our custodians take the stand that I'm free to wander and preach as long as I wander and preach outside their particular jurisdiction. They escort me to the border, quite often kick me in the seat, and tell me not to come back."

Justin moistened his lips. "Haven't you ever been on the—Conveyor?"

"Conveyor, William? Oh yes. You mean that strange new sacrament of theirs?"

Sacrament? Well, that was one thing you could call it with its element of penance and confession. Another was sadistic lunacy, systematic starvation, drugging and torture designed to exact a meaningless "confession" which everybody knew was worthless. Perhaps it was a dark sacrament after all, intelligible only to faith.

Mr. Sparhawk was saying: "Yes, I've been on the Conveyor. But what did I have to confess? They gave up after three days."

"They won't give up in MVD territory," Justin said grimly. "You were a fool to move in here. Did you think they were gone by now?"

"My dear fellow, of course I didn't. It was a Test."

A Test. Justin went silently to the corner and pried up a floorboard. Under it was the last bottle of the Konreid brandy, a pint in a former cleaning-fluid bottle. A Test, he thought. A Test of manhood, patriotism, sanity——

"Do you drink?" he asked Mr. Sparhawk.

"Only natural wine," the old man apologized. "It is a clear contravention of the intended mission of alcohol to drink fortified wines or distilled liquors. But please don't let my presence stop you from indulging."

"It won't," Justin said flatly. He knew Gribble's eyes were on the bottle in his hand, hungrily hoping. He poured a glassful for the little man and shoved it at him. He himself drank from the bottle, carefully, and put it in his pocket. The raw liquor cut like a file and he felt the dizziness of intoxication almost at once. Careful, he said sharply to himself. Get brave if you have to but don't become a drunken fool. He asked Mr. Sparhawk: "What do you mean by Test?"

"Why, William, a Test is a Test. A trial, an assay—I don't really know how to answer. But every once in a while one must prove that he isn't relapsing into sloth and merely mumbling words. One must *do* something, deliberately and knowing it will be difficult, dangerous, disagreeable. Surely you understand. That's why I entered territory under the direction of the Ministry of Internal Affairs. It's quite a good Test, too. Not *nasty*, like Saint What's-her-name swallowing tubercular sputum. When people do that sort of thing, there's always the possibility that some confounded Freudian is going to call them lunatics. Oh, a good Test is hard to find, William! I flatter myself that I've found one in our green-clothed friends' rigorous enforcement of the occupation statutes . . ."

While the old man rambled on, it suddenly became crystal-clear to Justin that he had all along been able to re-establish communications with the bomb plot.

All he had to do now, all he'd needed to do all along, was walk out and do it.

First try walking to Washington, Pennsylvania, to find the Bee-Jay salesman.

If that failed, as it might, he should walk to the senator's home town in Michigan and inquire around.

If that didn't work, he should walk to Washington, D.C., and find out what was going on in the Fish and Wild Life Survey.

If none of these worked, he would have to try some of the more tenuous clues.

There were certain objections to the scheme, he realized. One was that he'd probably be arrested before he got a mile beyond Norton, New York. This would probably lead to his torture, confession, and execution unless he used his razor blade in time. But he smiled incredulously at himself for once having thought that this objection overruled the need to walk out and re-establish contact so that the ghost satellite could be sent up.

If Mr. Sparhawk could take the beatings and the uncertainty in exchange for his urge to wander and preach, what shouldn't *he* be able to accept and risk with nothing less at stake than the nation?

It was as simple as that. If you have to walk out and do it, the way to do it is to walk out and do it.

And the first thing to do was disobey his first command: not to be taken alive.

"Mr. Sparhawk," he said abruptly, "your time on the Conveyor—is there anything you did so you kept from breaking down? Have you got sedatives or anything like that?"

The old man said: "I must confess I used Yoga—abused it, rather, for the use it is to abuse it. Yoga is, of course, a set of philosophical systems intended to put one beyond identity and desire, but the Conveyor is peculiarly persuasive that one has an identity and desires to retain in." He chuckled complacently. "Asana postures are effective while confined in a cell waiting. It is part of their scheme to break one down by waiting. The soul which does not seek release from the Wheel is prey to terrors and fancies during such an interlude. However, I would assume the siddhasana, thus——" Mr. Sparhawk squirmed into a Buddha-like posture which outraged Justin's training as an artist in that it went far beyond the bounds of what his anatomy textbooks regarded as possible to a human being.

"And I would vary it with the padmasana, thus——" Mr. Sparhawk squirmed again, and this time settled down into a position which looked possible but exquisitely uncomfortable. "The postures," said Mr. Sparhawk, "have carried me through a bit of solitary confinement. They use dark cells, you know, and that's the sort of thing that drives most chaps absolutely crackers. And there's pranayama, of course." He seemed to have finished.

"Pranayama?" Justin urged gently.

"Oh, you don't know about it, do you?" asked the old man disapprovingly. "It's the yoga of breathing, and quite important. I used it when they were beating me a bit. You see, one breathes in through the left nostril seven and a half seconds and holds it for thirty and a half seconds. One then expels through the right nostril in fifteen and a half seconds, then inhales through the same nostril for the same period, then one——"

"And this—helped?"

"How could it fail to, William? During pranayama one is sometimes so freed of distractions that one floats about the room, though I admit I've not done that yet or seen it. Surely a truncheon across the shins could be only a minor nuisance to one deeply engaged in pranayama, don't you think?"

"As long as it works."

Sparhawk sighed regretfully: "William, old man, I can see you're struggling with it as a difficult idea. If only you were a bit along in Zen, how simple it would be! I'd merely kick you in the bum by surprise or unexpectedly shout "Fiddle-dee-dee!' in your ear and it would all come to you. What a mess you've made of your life, William. No Zen at all. The time you've wasted!"

Justin clenched his fists and said: "I'm not going to waste any more time, Mr. Sparhawk. Take me with you."

The old man asked coldly, suddenly alert, "Is this what you call a rib, William?"

"I'm perfectly sincere. I want to go with you. To Washington, Pennsylvania."

"My dear boy, it doesn't matter where one goes. But I'm afraid a vestigial attachment to worldly vanities keeps me from enjoying this joke of yours. If you'll excuse me, I must say my prayers and turn in."

"He means it!" Gribble suddenly squalled,

terrified. "Don't leave me, Justin, don't leave me alone here, they'll beat me up to find out where you went and they'll shoot me in the cellar——"

"Work it out for yourself, Gribble," Justin said gently. "I'm going. I've got to. Tell them any lies you like and if they don't work, die like a man. *Before you tell the truth.*"

Sparhawk rose from his padmasana posture, excitement in his eyes. "You do mean it, William?" he asked tremulously. "This isn't a joke?"

Justin said: "I'm not joking. Not about risking my life. I want to go with you."

And, he said to himself, *by this token you cease to be a peasant, an animal. It's important that you set out on your military mission, of course. But it's important that you set out on any mission at all and by that token become once more a man.*

"Mr. Sparhawk," he said diffidently. The old man was silently praying, but turned to smile beatifically at him. "Mr. Sparhawk, I know you make a point of early departure, but could we stay here until mail time tomorrow? I want to say good-by."

"I understand." The old man beamed at his convert. "I think we can permit it."

Good-by, Betsy Cardew. What might have been will never be.

CHAPTER SIXTEEN

They had been five days on the road and covered twenty miles as the crow flies, eighty on the back roads chosen from an old Texaco map, when they met their first Reds.

Sparhawk was drilling Justin when it happened; they were in a quiet clearing outside Leona, Pennsylvania, which the old man thought suitable for contemplation.

Justin, under his direction, contorted himself into the joint-wrenching padmasana and was trying not to snicker at the order which followed. It was to look at the space between his eyebrows and meditate upon the syllable "Om." The soldiers, a ten-man squad, came out of the woods at that point.

The soldiers looked at them and roared

with laughter. Their sergeant and Mr. Sparhawk were able to converse after a fashion in mixed English and Russian. Justin did not succeed in looking at the space between his eyebrows or in meditating upon the syllable "Om." Locked in the padmasana, he watched the parley between the two men and meditated on the Conveyor. From time to time one of the soldiers would poke him curiously and grin: *"Galyootsinahtsya."*

The parley ended; the soldiers left. The tremendous fact was that they had been intercepted, had been unable to show documents justifying their presence, and yet had not been arrested.

"How did you do it, Mr. Sparhawk?" he gasped.

"Satagraha," Mr. Sparhawk said absently. "Soul force. It works, you know. Most of the time, that is. Their tendency is to assume that one's probably all right and that anyway it's no business of theirs. Marked contrast with the MVDs, whose assumption is that one probably isn't all right and that everything's business of theirs. But let's not chatter, William. You're supposed to be in the padmasana. Supposed to be, I say with reason. What is the padmasana? It is the right foot on the left thigh, the left foot on the right thigh, holding the right great toe with the right hand, the left great toe with the left hand, the hands coming from behind the back and crossing, the chin resting on the interclavicular space, the sight fixed on the space between the eyebrows—failing that, the tip of

the nose. In one respect you succeed, William, you have managed to look at the tip of your nose. You must try harder."

Justin, his eyes aching from being crossed on his nose, his neck aching, his thighs and arms and back aching, tried harder. Mr. Sparhawk slid easily into the posture and went on: "When the command of padmasana has been attained, you will find there is no longer suffering from cold, heat, hunger, thirst, fatigue, or similar afflictions . . ."

It was nice that the old man believed it all, Justin thought as he ached. His belief, even expressed in pigdin Russian, shone transcendently through the words and had got the pair of them tacitly certified as harmless lunatics.

Their second week on the road, trending generally southwest into the Allegheny Valley, found them one night approaching a run-down farmhouse. There was no light to be seen. A starving mongrel dog snapped at them when they climbed to the littered, unswept porch; Justin drove him off with a stick while Mr. Sparhawk rapped politely on the door. There was no answer. Mr. Sparhawk rapped again and the unlatched door swung open, creaking. By moonlight through a window they saw an old man sprawled on the floor.

Mr. Sparhawk took over with crisp efficiency. Pulse, skin, and a hoarse rattle in the chest told him, he said, that the man was suffering pneumonia and starvation. They brought the cot from his bedroom into the kitchen and built a roaring fire in the stove. They made gruel and spooned some down the sick man's throat, and for a couple of hours while they watched he seemed to rally. He died at midnight, though, and they buried him in the morning in his backyard. Justin had to keep driving off the dog and was careful to put a layer of heavy stones on the grave.

The weather was hardly brisk yet—at least to men who had been through the war years on scant fuel rations. The old man must have been ready to go from the first bug that got into his system. But it was a foretaste of the coming winter, which would do the Reds' work thoroughly and well. It would kill Americans by the million, and would leave open to settlement new acres by the million.

Who said there were no continents left to discover? A dozen winters would come and go, and finally the Russians would come and find a land almost as bare of humanity as Columbus had.

While Mr. Sparhawk whispered a meditation of St. John of the Cross by the graveside, Justin methodically searched the farmhouse and struck gold. A hard lump in the old man's pillow turned out to be a tin box crammed with sewing needles, thread, razor blades, and a can of black pepper. He distributed the treasures among his pockets and returned to the grave, where he joined in the meditation.

The signpost said they were three miles from Clarion and the map said this was a town of some size lying astride an interstate highway. It was to be avoided. They had lost a week traveling by a stop to get in the corn crop of a sick old couple. They worked from sunrise to sunset for seven days, and when the golden ears were neatly stored in the cribs, were told they were a pair of heathen and had better git before they got the law put on them.

"Rub of the green, William," Mr. Sparhawk said philosophically as they trudged away.

Justin was glad to get away on any terms. The work had been nothing to him; he was inured to fatigue and hunger. The lost week had been agony, every hour of it. Finally Mr. Sparhawk was forced to say gently: "Washington, Pennsylvania, won't run away, William. Surely we are doing as much good here as we could do there?"

And that meant *shut up*. There Justin had to leave it. It was barely possible that the old man might continue to tolerate his presence, might even act as a cover story if he knew that Justin was using him to establish communications with a revolutionary army. It was certain that he could not do it without losing his appearance of blissful sincerity and gentle mania which had carried them through every brush with the occupation.

It was three miles out of Clarion, perhaps halfway on the road to Washington, Pennsylvania, that they met the kid gang. They leaped on Justin and Mr. Sparhawk from the roadside; perhaps some of them swung down cinematically from tree limbs. There may have been two dozen of them, between eight and fifteen years of age. They gave the two travelers the treatment they gave all travelers whom they surprised and outnumbered; they beat and kicked them viciously, robbed them, stripped them to their underwear and moved on, laughing and shoving. Mr. Sparhawk after moving his jaw tentatively mumbled between bruised lips: "You did well not to resist, William. Such groups have been known to kill."

"I couldn't resist, damn it!" Justin snorted. "The little demons were all over me. I'd like to meet just four of them in a dark alley sometime. I think I've got a couple of broken ribs——"

He and Mr. Sparhawk helped each other to get up; they hobbled down the road.

"Look," Justin said, alarmed, "this'll take us to Clarion. Township seat, ten thousand people, a Red garrison for sure. Let's figure a detour."

"We must *find* a garrison of the occupying forces," Mr. Sparhawk said serenely. "We must report this incident. We owe it to those boys; we must stop them before they do irreparable damage to their souls. I have, thank God, been privileged to report five such wandering bands and each one was rounded up within a day or two. Whatever penalties were exacted from them, they were at least stopped in their careers."

The mad reasoning on alien values would work. Justin knew it. They would be two lunatics wandering into town half naked in late October, gently and without acrimony urging that the authorities pick up the kid gang without ado—for the good of their souls.

On to Clarion, Pennsylvania.

Early November brought a cold snap and wet, heavy snow. They were floundering, calf-deep, by afternoon along a black-top between Leechburg and North Vandegrift, about two hundred miles beeline from Norton, about fifty miles from Washington, Pennsylvania. It was clear that the journey would soon be over. Justin had lost twenty pounds and gained an impatient respect for Mr. Sparhawk's innocent tenacity.

He had seen a countryside under lock and key, reverting sullenly to the ancient peasant status never known before on the continent. They had by-passed manufacturing towns—Mr. Sparhawk believed in reasonable caution until his disciple's spiritual qualities were more highly developed—and so had not seen the worst.

A woman in an ancient Model A sedan stopped and called to them. "Want a lift, boys?" It was the first time this had happened in their month on the road. She had a gas-ration sticker on her windshield and the trunk of the car, which *was* a trunk and not a streamlined cavern, stood half open. It was crammed with canned goods.

The woman was fat, red-faced, and smiling. Strangely, her fat was not the waxy, loosely attached "potato fat" of an all-starch diet; it was firm plumpness. In that famine year, it meant villainy.

"No thank you, madam," Justin said automatically.

Beside him Mr. Sparhawk looked mulish. "I think we ought to, William," he said gently. "Madame, we'll be pleased to ride with you." Resignedly Justin got in.

She outtalked Mr. Sparhawk for ten miles. She was the widowed Mrs. Elphinstone. She had a farm worked by six good-for-nothing orphans she boarded for the county out of the goodness of her heart. She didn't believe in saying anything about a person if you couldn't say anything good, *but*——

It was common knowledge about the Baptist preacher and Miss Lesh.

But that shouldn't surprise you because *Mister* Lesh had died in a madhouse even if they called it a rest home. When it's in the blood, there's nothing you can do.

Mr. Tebbets, the lawyer, was drunk again when she was in town.

Everybody knew he bought it from Mrs. Grassman, whose husband drank himself to death on home brew, and somebody should tell the authorities before more damage was done.

But it was probably Mr. Tebbets' conscience that drove him to drink, the way he swindled the Murdocks out of their insurance money.

Not that Tebbets was the worst of the gang; she wasn't a prude, dear no, but the way his crony Dr. Reeves carried on before right-minded people ran him out of town, why she herself knew a girl who had been given gas by

Dr. Reeves for an extraction and woke to find her brassiere unhooked.

Though it was hard to see why the little slut—it was Margie Endicott—should care, since every boy in the senior high had done at least as much.

And if the truth were known—

She saw a couple walking along the road and stopped the car. They were a farmer and his wife; each carried a sack. "Hello, Elsie," the man said nervously. His wife looked murder and said nothing.

"Why, Ralph and Kate, imagine running into you here! Where you going?"

"Little walk," the man muttered.

The woman was staring at their sacks, licking her lips. "The Ladies," she said, "are getting up a little luncheon, I meant to tell you. Times being what they are, we're all chipping in on the eatables. You're invited of course, Kate." Her voice became shrill and childish. "Now I was just wondering if you'd like to save a trip by handing over any little thing you have with you—for the Ladies."

"We haven't got anything," the farmer's wife said sharply.

"My goodness, isn't that too bad? I heard somebody around your way butchered a hog and I thought you might have some old scraps of it. For the Ladies."

The farmer rummaged in his sack and pulled out a four-pound flitch of bacon. Naked hatred was in his eyes. He chucked it into the car beside the woman. "Come on," he said to his wife flatly. She shouldered her sack and they walked on through the swirling snow.

Justin knew he was riding with a woman who one of these days would be murdered.

She started the car. "The Perkinsons," she said. "Worthless, lawless trash. I've got half a mind to tell Lieutenant Sokoloff they've been butchering without a permit—but forevermore, who doesn't?" She turned around as she drove to smile at her passengers. "What I say is the important thing is not to get caught at it." The car eased into the right-hand roadside ditch before she turned back to her driving; she squawked, spun the wheels and killed the motor.

"Isn't that awful? I wonder if you'd boys try what you can do. I'll just stay here in case you need help from the engine——"

They got out in the snow and heaved and looked for rocks to lay as a tread under the spinning wheels and from time to time asked her to try driving out. They got snow spun into their faces and bruised their fingers on frozen rocks. They talked in whispers. The woman's ruddy face was hanging out the window; she was watching with interest.

"Blackmailing old——"

"Steady on, William."

"We shouldn't have got in the car."

"Is *her* salvation unimportant for some reason known to you? We must give each person we meet his or her chance."

"The only way you can save that type is with a firing squad. The neighborhood gossip, the village terror, hand in hand with the Reds.

She'll get hers the way Croley's going to."

"Mr. Croley has been charitable to me."

"Sure. Croley's smart enough to play *all* the sides—not like her." Justin pounded a rock under the wheel with another rock. "Give her a try, ma'am," he said aloud.

"I certainly hope it works, boys," she said. "I'm getting awfully chilly." She roared the motor, let in her clutch, and was off in a shower of slush and small stones.

Justin waited for her to stop on the road for them but she chugged on. When the Ford vanished around a distant curve, he did some swearing and wound up: "At least we don't have to listen to her any more."

"No," Mr. Sparhawk said, and for a moment Justin thought the look he gave him was compassionate.

The woman must have hurried home and put in a phone call. Half an hour later a pair of Red jeeps overtook them. An hour later they were being booked for sabotage, counter-revolutionary wrecking, and sedition in what had once been the principal's office of the Leechburg Consolidated School.

The next day they were on the Conveyor.

Justin sat in the dark and absently rubbed his aching neck. The session had lasted for six hours, and Lieutenant Sokoloff had been yawning at the end of it. It was not surprising; Sokoloff was merely a cop and he himself was merely a vagrant against whom a routine accusation had been brought. Sokoloff would sleep now for eight hours; Justin would be

kept awake and presumably irritated just
below the threshold of pain by irregular
switching on and off of the lights, peering
guards with raucous orders, the steel-pipe
bunk without bedding, to corrugate his back.

Then, rested and refreshed, Sokoloff would
plump himself into a padded swivel chair,
Justin would sit bolt upright on a too-low
stool, the dazzling light would be switched on,
and the interrogation would proceed.

The bright cell lights flashed on and a
soldier's heavy face peered through the bars.
He pounded on them with a night stick and
growled, "Prisoner hobey hord-erss," and
stood waiting. Justin obediently went and lay
down on the steel-pipe cot, face up, hands at
his side, and closed his eyes. The light beat
through his eyelids. The transverse pipes bit
into his heel tendons, his calfs, thighs,
buttocks, back, neck, and skull. Orders were
being obeyed. He was not being physically tor-
tured. He was merely lying on a bunk, what in
heaven's name could you expect to find in a
detention cell? Their strange passion for
legality again—a sort of legality, at least.

It showed up strongly in the questions
during interrogation. Justin was at sea
several times until he inferred the hypothesis
behind such a question as: "Did the prisoner
ever take part in the workers' struggle before
organized assistance to the clandestine
N.A.P.D.R. began to arrive?" What Sokoloff
wanted to know was had Justin been a
Communist before the war. Justin had not
been a Communist before the war, and if he

answered "No" to the question as Sokoloff phrased it, he was saying a great deal more than he had not been a Communist before the war. He was admitting Sokoloff's premise about "organized assistance to the clandestine N.A.P.D.R." He was agreeing with Sokoloff that the war was not a war of aggression at all but an internal revolution by the Communist Party with some assistance from the Soviet Union and the Chinese People's Republic. Therefore he could not answer such questions yes or no, and therefore Sokoloff became very angry and turned the light that glared in his eyes brighter. But that wasn't torture, of course. Could one expect an interrogation room to function without a light by which notes could be jotted and the expression of the prisoner observed?

Justin didn't know where Mr. Sparhawk was except that he was in some place exactly like this, or what he was doing except that it was exactly what Justin was doing: hanging on.

A sacrament, Mr. Sparhawk called it, innocently blasphemous.

"Is the prisoner aware that to absent oneself from one's assigned agricultural holdings is sabotage of food production?"

"Spreading the Word of God comes first, Lieutenant Sokoloff. Under the guarantees of religious freedom of the North American People's Democratic Republic no functionary is empowered to interfere with the private or public worship of a religious body."

The passion for legality cut both ways.

"The prisoner is not a religious body!"

"I consider myself the disciple of Mr. Sparhawk, Lieutenant Sokoloff, and I consider Mr. Sparhawk a lay preacher."

"What is the name of your religion?"

"It has no name. It incorporates what Mr. Sparhawk finds inspired in all religions."

"There are no such religions. The prisoner is a poseur. Is the prisoner aware that he has been denounced as a counter-revolutionary wrecker by a loyal adherent of the N.A.P.D.R., to whom he has made inflammatory and seditious speeches?"

"If you please, Lieutenant, I made no speeches to the lady you mean. I would have spoken to her about God—but I never got the chance."

Sokoloff's face, dim on the fringes of the dazzling interrogation light, wrinkled into a brief grin. He knew the lady, then.

And so it went for six hours, the two of them pounding each other with stuffed clubs labeled respectively SABOTAGE and FREEDOM OF WORSHIP.

Justin shifted on the bunk, acutely uncomfortable. That was supposed to be Lieutenant Sokoloff's margin of victory. The lieutenant would rest well, he would not rest at all. The next session he would swing his padded club with less vigor while Sokoloff's blows would be as strong as ever. At last, after a week or so of interrupted sleep, scanty meals, inflamed eyelids, and backache, Lieutenant Sokoloff would be flailing away as hard as ever and he would sit apathetically, without the strength or spirit to strike a blow. He would sign anything, admit anything, to sleep on a cement floor instead of the steel-pipe bunk.

In theory.

He tried one of Mr. Sparhawk's heathen tricks which had served him on rainy nights before. He willed his muscles to relax one by one, from his toes up. He sent out his will to gather up his aches into a ball twelve inches in diameter and he floated the ball twelve inches above his forehead, where he could inspect it impersonally. The distractions kept trying to crowd in, but he succeeded in keeping them out by not giving a damn about them. When the ball slowly began to sag down and threatened to re-enter his body, he thought relaxedly that to do so would result in the discovery of the bombardment satellite and that therefore the ball should continue to float. It did, and he slept. Much better than young Lieutenant Sokoloff, who was tossing and turning and worrying about what to do with these lunatics he had been saddled with by that horrible woman.

The private ceremoniously kicked Mr. Sparhawk in the seat, booting him over the township line. Justin, moving fast, stepped across without assistance. They started down the road.

Behind them Lieutenant Sokoloff, dark bags under his eyes, yelled: "And don't you ever come back into this area again, do you hear me?"

Mr. Sparhawk turned and waved. "Yes,

Lieutenant. God bless you."

They heard the jeep start up and roar away.

They had been five days on the Conveyor. They were skin and bones; their backs and buttocks were covered with bruises from all the hours spent rigid on the pipe bunks and hard interrogation light and the lights in their cells. They were filthy; it was part of the system to allow no water for washing and thereby further break down the morale of the prisoner. Mr. Sparhawk's left thumb and index finger were broken and splinted; a guard, strictly against orders, had whacked him with his night stick. Six of Justin's molars had been pulled; the unit dentist had examined them, decided fillings were needed, and done considerable drilling before further deciding they could not be saved after all. She had done her work without anesthetic and Lieutenant Sokoloff had stood by to distract the prisoner by chatting about the pleasures of the pretrial cells, which were furnished with regular army cots. These pretrial cells were only for prisoners who had cleared all preliminary hurdles, such as the signing of confessions.

His jaws ached horribly, he had ridden the Conveyor for five days and they were walking into the town of Washington, Pennsylvania.

CHAPTER SEVENTEEN

They signed in first thing in the Transients book of the local SMGU. They explained to a puzzled English-speaking sergeant that they were ministers of the gospel and that he might check with his neighboring SMGU, where, through a misunderstanding, they had been detained, interrogated, and cleared. Then—it was about noon—they made their pitch on a busy corner of the main shopping street.

Mr. Sparhawk lectured on Conscience and Submission; Justin borrowed a hat and passed it. One of the people who dropped in coins was the salesman from Bee-Jay. "Meet me later," Justin muttered. The man gave him a brief appraising stare and walked away.

After the lecture they almost quarreled. Justin was for finding a rooming house with a bath and taking a week's lodgings. Mr. Sparhawk, now that Justin's irrational desire to see Washington, Pennsylvania, had been gratified, was for a one-day stay mostly devoted to preaching.

They had dinner in a tavern, Mr. Sparhawk relenting to the point of taking a glass of watery beer and allowing Justin one. But no matter how longingly the disciple eyed the steam table of sausages and roast horse meat, they ate the vegetable plate.

The dispute was still unresolved when they checked in at a rooming house down near the railroad tracks. Justin's jaws were aching badly but he didn't care. The Bee-Jay salesman had passed by the tavern and glanced in while they were eating. The contact had not been broken. Surely they were being followed and marked . . .

They bathed in turn, very gratefully, and turned in. Mr. Sparhawk slept on the floor and laughed when Justin offered him the bed. Justin understood the laughter an hour later while he tossed and turned and angrily commanded his muscles to relax. He had made up his mind at last to spread a blanket on the floor and sleep there himself when he heard a scratching on the door.

The long ordeal was ended.

He opened up. It was the Bee-Jay salesman, of course, and two other men. They all wore coveralls and carried telephone linemen's gear in broad leather belts.

"Come along," the salesman said softly. "We have a truck. And guns."

He assumed they would have guns. "We don't have to wake up the old man," he whispered to one of them who was stooping over Mr. Sparhawk.

"He's coming," the man said, and shook him.

"Friends of mine, Mr. Sparhawk," Justin whispered. "We're taking a short trip."

"Yeah," said the salesman. He raised his hand. "No arguments. Explain everything later."

"I never argue," Mr. Sparhawk whispered loftily, and they dressed and went quietly down the stairs, the salesman in front of them and the two strangers behind. The truck was an olive-green A.T.&T. cab-over-engine repair job, the kind of truck that can appear anywhere on the continent without a word of comment or stir of interest as long as there is a telephone within fifty miles. Justin was struck by the brilliant simplicity of the idea. When they were settled in the dark body of the truck with the two strangers, he started to say as much. They told him to be quiet. He didn't like their manner, but set it down to the strain of a risky mission.

Mr. Sparhawk settled down on the floor in the padmasana posture while the truck bumped over a lot of railroad tracks and made a lot of left and right turns and a couple of U turns that could only have been meant to confuse their sense of direction. In half an hour the truck stopped definitely, the hand brake rasped along its ratchets, and the motor stopped.

They hustled Justin and Mr. Sparhawk out of the truck onto a dimly lit loading deck of concrete. Down a concrete corridor where fork hoists and stacks of pallets stood. Past a thousand stacked new milk cans shining dully. Past crates of pitcher pumps and a thousand cream separators. Into a concrete room where a dozen men awaited them. When the door rolled shut behind them, Justin weakly said, "I'm glad to see you." But he already knew that it was no joyful reunion but a trial.

"Now we can talk," the Bee-Jay salesman said grimly.

"Yes," said Justin between his teeth. Then he yelled at them: "Why was Chiunga County deserted?"

Their faces were shocked. The trapped mouse had turned and bit them on the finger.

"Not that you give a damn," Justin said, "But Chiunga happens to be the key to the whole situation, as you'd know if your organization were conducted sensibly. Why haven't we had any couriers? Why don't you answer us on the dry wire? Why were we left to rot?"

"While we're asking questions, William," Mr. Sparhawk said mildly, "what on earth are you talking about?"

They ignored him. The Bee-Jay salesman said slowly: "You might as well know my name, Justin. Sam Lowenthal. I used to be a civilian consultant to the psychological-warfare branch. You don't have to know who all these people are. It's enough to say that they constitute a court-martial of the United States Army. You're on trial for treason. We suspect you of being a stool pigeon, Justin. We thought so when we got a dry-wire message that somebody named Justin had important information for a top contact team. We sent in the team—and never heard from it again.

"Now we find you here in a fairly important subheadquarters town after a 250-mile journey. People don't make such journeys nowadays—not unless they're helped either by us or their friends the Reds. And we know we didn't help you. And with you is an unexplained person."

That was with a jerk of the thumb at Mr. Sparhawk, who had indignantly withdrawn into the padmasana. Justin could see from the shape of his mouth that he was meditating on the syllable "Om."

"And once you're here you brazenly try to make contact with us. Our idea, Justin, is that this is a naïve attempt—motivated by Marxist fantacism, perhaps—to infiltrate our group and put the finger on us for the Reds. If you have anything to say, speak up—but I suspect you're going to wind up tonight in the Bee-Jay fertilizer division."

The first thing Justin did was take off his shirt. They gasped at the bruises and sores. He told them: "They also drilled my teeth for six hours the other day. Can any of you comfortable masterminds say as much? No, I didn't break. That's because I've learned a great many things from the eccentric gentleman sitting in the corner there. One of them was patience and another was recklessness. You people could use some of both.

"I believe you when you tell me the senator and his two friends disappeared after they interviewed me. People are disappearing all the time in this year of grace. I presume they used their razor blades before they were questioned, so my information died with them. Now listen to it this time.

"*Yankee Doodle* was a diversionary dummy. The real ghost satellite, about 99 per cent completed, is under Prospect Hill in Chiunga County in a limestone cavern. It needs electronics men and electronics parts. It needs an ace rocket-intercepter pilot. It needs a missile team with plenty of background in math. Of course, if you people would rather spend your time holed up comfortably worrying about stool pigeons, that's your business; I'm not running your campaign for you."

Lowenthal was stunned by the outburst. He said shakily: "I used to hear a rumor when I was detached to the AEC—listen, Justin. We'll quarantine you and pass the matter up higher for a decision as soon as possible——"

Justin put on his shirt and turned to the door.

"Justin!" Lowenthal snapped, pulling out a .45 pistol.

"Yes?" Justin asked mildly.

"Where do you think you're going?"

"Out."

"I'll kill you if you take another step toward the door."

"I suppose you will. Why should that stop me? Don't you realize I was supposed to be shot for walking 250 miles to listen to your drivel about passing it up for a decision? Hell, man, I wasn't supposed to get past one township line, let alone fifty! I was supposed to be shot for storing that hunk of A-bomb you picked up at my place. I was supposed to be shot for not reporting the top contact crew you sent. I was supposed to be shot for not turning over the bombardment satellite to the Reds as fast as my scared little legs could carry me.

"Go ahead and shoot, man. But if you don't, if by some chance I get out of here, I'm going to rustle up some electronics men, some parts, and a crew while you good people are waiting for a decision from higher up. Good-by."

He started for the door again. Lowenthal's pistol slide went back with a click and forward with a thud. "Wait," the psychologist said when Justin put his hand on the door.

"What do you want?" Justin demanded.

"I think," Lowenthal said slowly, "you may have a valid point. Perhaps we do sometimes display a little less divine madness than we ought to—suppose, Justin, I send you off to Chiunga County in a sealed freight car tomorrow with our Dr. Dace. He's the head of research and development for Bee-Jay. We can arrange a breakdown from overwork for him."

Justin snapped: "Is your Dr. Dace a satellite crew, a team of electronics men, and half a ton of equipment?"

Dace himself, small, peppery, white-haired, and mean-eyed, got up and snarled, "You arrogant pup, who the hell do you think you are to survey a bombardment satellite? 'Half a ton of equipment'—do you think that's the same as half a ton of candy bars? Now sit down and shut up while we plan this thing through." He suddenly looked conscience-stricken and added lamely: "Er, naturally we all appreciate the, uh, heroism you displayed in making the very arduous trip you did to re-establish contact with us . . ." He trailed off and sat down.

The discussion became general and complicated. After a while Lowenthal dismissed four men who seemed to have nothing to contribute on the technical side. Justin suspected they were to have been the firing squad.

Dace relentlessly probed Justin's every recollection of the satellite's appearance and scribbled notes. Lowenthal tsk-tsk'd because Justin had left Gribble on his own.

"What should I have done?" Justin demanded.

Lowenthal hesitated. "Maybe parked him in the cave. Or killed him."

Justin found himself on his feet raving: "God help the human race if you thugs are its fighters for liberty. If we kill a man like Gribble in the name of security how are we different from the Reds or the Chinese? We don't even have the excuses they have of ignorance and oppression and hunger. What kind of cowards are you that you'd kill a sick man so you won't have to worry about betrayal?"

"Take it easy," Lowenthal said. "You'll kill before this is over." Justin sat down, shaking. He knew he would. He also knew the psychologist was deliberately missing the point.

A little information about the rebellion as a whole seeped out of the general discussion. Justin could gather that there were many areas which had been quarantined like Chiunga County as too dangerous to work into the scheme. Elsewhere they had the dry wires, postmen, and traveling salesmen for communication. They had seeded professional soldiers across the country— Rawson was Chiunga County's leader-to-be.

The situation in the great cities was either they were very strong at a given time or they were wiped out. The cities offered countless hiding places where arms could be stored and food cached and plans made. They offered countless volunteers—among whom were traitors. There were many people in the cities who had responded to the relentless psychological pressure of Red propaganda and thought they were sincere, idealistic Marxists. It was impossible to say without the latest word from the wires whether they had a working organization or a demoralized corporal's guards in, for instance, New York. The organization in New York City had collapsed five times and risen six. Thousands had been shot in roundups; there were always thousands more to recruit.

"We don't think," Lowenthal said slowly, "the Reds realize the magnitude of it. They're hypnotized by their fable of "counter-revolutionary wrecking.' This handicaps them in dealing with the real situation. That's how the Nazis were handicapped in dealing with underground organizations throughout Europe during World War Two. They were thunderstruck when the French underground recaptured Paris before the Allied troops arrived."

"But the Allied troops were on their way," Justin said pointedly.

"You're right. Perhaps I should have cited the uprising of the Warsaw ghetto, where the remnants of the original population organized and supplied an army that held the Nazis at bay for ten days. I had uncles and cousins in Warsaw; I've often wondered since I got into this thing whether they fought in the uprising or whether they were shipped to an extermination camp before it happened."

Justin had been in high school during that war. "How did the uprising come out?" he asked.

"They were killed to the last man, woman, and child," Lowenthal said, surprised. "The ghetto was pounded into gravel by artillery."

Dr. Dace snapped: "I'm sick and tired of your Warsaw Concerto, Sam. Let's get on with the work."

But after a while they were talking again.

Justin learned that nobody there knew where Headquarters were, that the Russian railroad inspectors were free-wheeling, happy-go-lucky types whom it was easy to hoodwink and possible to bribe, that so far nobody had succeeded in corrupting an MVD man.

The situation across the Mississippi, under the Chinese, was more urgent that it was in the East under the Russians. The ancient Chinese contempt for human life led to executions for such things as smoking in public. There was some sort of decree posted everywhere in which every American was placed under suspended sentence of death for banditry and terrorism; any noncommissioned officer could execute the sentence for reasons which seemed sufficient to him. However, the language difference made organization and communication much easier. If the American cringed to the color-conscious invader, the invader was happy enough about that gratifying fact to neglect training sufficient officers in the difficult English language to police the mails and wires.

Somebody had a watch and announced that it was four-thirty and he for one wanted some sleep.

"One last item," said Dace. "What about him? That was Mr. Sparhawk, sleeping soundly on the concrete floor. The old man woke up at once and asked mildly: "What about me?"

"I'd like him to come along with us in the freight car," Justin said. "We can keep him in the cave."

"Freight car?" said Mr. Sparhawk disdainfully. "William, how am I supposed to preach and teach in a freight car? You're acting awfully strange, I must say. I had no particular objections about coming to this town, because after all one must go somewhere. But now a freight car and a cave? Too foolish!"

Dr. Dace said: "I've heard about this egg. He preaches submission. Furthermore, he's nuts. I say rub him out."

"What a savage little man you are," Mr. Sparhawk said wonderingly. "You know, it's all very well to talk, but violence won't do. I was a colonel in the Brigade of Guards, gentlemen; I know what I'm saying."

"What *are* you saying?" Dace bristled.

"Why, that I saw the Guards break under the Russian armored attack on Salisbury Plain. I saw the capture of the Royal Family with my own eyes. Her Majesty, of course, was superb. But—it *was* defeat, you know. That was when I discovered there was a basic mistake. If the Guards could be broken and Her Majesty captured, *obviously* we'd been mistaken all along with our guns and rockets and bombs and the answer lay elsewhere. Since then I've been seeking it, gentlemen——"

"Mr. Sparhawk," Justin said, "I wish you'd come along. I couldn't have got this far without you. I don't know whether I can finish it without you."

"You want me for a mascot?" the old man

asked wryly.

"Not a mascot. As—as a chaplain, I suppose," Justin said.

"Well—I'll come along," Mr. Sparhawk said. "As a chaplain. You bloody-minded individuals can use some spiritual ministration in any case."

Justin, without knowing why, felt immensely relieved. More, he had the impression that everybody else in the concrete storeroom was too.

CHAPTER EIGHTEEN

"Where the hell have you been?" demanded Gus Feinblatt in an angry whisper.

They were in front of Croley's store in Norton; Justin had walked down for sign-in day. The MVD *starsheey syterjahnt* was presiding inside the store over the book. Men and women apathetically walked in from time to time, found their place on the page, and signed. Then they stood around, or bought something, or just walked out.

"Where the hell were you last sign-in? For that matter, where the hell have you been ai month?" whispered Feinblatt. "We had Stan Potocki sign in for you. When we found you were gone and that nut Gribble of yours couldn't tell us anything, we had Stan practice for a week and then come in with a bunch of us early to sign for himself and another bunch late to sign for you. We could have been shot! You just shouldn't have done it, Billy!''

''I had to,'' Justin said. ''Thanks, Gus.'' He reached into his pocket and found a penny, a steel disk with a wreathed star on one side and the head of Tom Paine on the other. ''Here,' he said. ''Christmas Eve.'' Gus took the penny automatically, looked bewildered, and Justin went into the store.

''Vot name?'' The sergeant scowled.

''Moyoh eemyah Yoostin,'' Billy said. *''Fermer.''*

The sergeant put his finger on the rectangle. He glanced at Justin and looked a little puzzled. Justin took the pen and looked at the signature above. It was a pretty bad imitation Potocki had done. With his trained fingers he imitated the imitation, trying not to *draw* the letters too obviously. It passed the sergeant's comparison. Whether it would pass the later, leisurely comparison of the headquarters officer who was at least a part-time hand-writing expert, he did not know.

Justin read a comic book—*Joe Hill, Hero of Labor*—for half an hour. At twelve noon a jeep came by for the sergeant; he closed his book grimly and drove off with it to the next hamlet down the line.

The store came to life then. Mr. Croley emerged from his cubbyhole to wait, dead pan, for customers to speak up. He sold some binder twine, fence staples, seed cake, cheese, imitation candy, and dark gray bread in a little flurry of business activity and then the store was empty again. Justin went to the counter.

"I'd like to talk in your office," he said. The storekeeper lifted the counter flap and went in first. "I hear you have some surplus stuff."

Croley sat at his small roll-top desk with the stuffed pigeon-holes and waited. Justin knew for what. He took out a bundle of money, big bills from Lowenthal's safe.

"Don't *have* any," Croley said. "Know where there *is* some, maybe. Big difference."

"Yeah. Big difference. Well, do you know where there might be some sacks of flour, dried peas, and beans? And case lots of canned horse meat, sugar, dried eggs, and tea?"

"Expensive stuff."

Justin spread out the bills in a fan.

Croley took them and said ritually: "I dunno for sure but I think maybe Mrs. Sprenger down past the gravel pit might be able to help you. I'll just write her a note about it."

He wrote a note to Mrs. Sprenger on the back of an old sales slip and sealed it with a blob of flour paste. Justin just got a glimpse, unavoidable in the tiny place unless he had turned his back, and saw that it seemed to be about flower seeds.

Croley handed him the note and Justin started to leave. Transaction over. End of incident. But amazingly Croley detained him. "Imagine you're getting around," the store-keeper said with a wintry little smile.

"Maybe," Justin said cautiously. So the old skunk was adding up his absence—he had noticed it of course; Croley noticed everything—and the big bills. Justin counted on Croley's own illegal part in the black-market transaction to keep his mouth shut. Counted too far?

But Croley said: "Anything I can do for you, let me know." *And shook his hand!*

In a daze Justin said, "Christmas Eve," and gave him a penny. Croley was looking at it in bewilderment as he left.

Justin thought he had Croley figured. The old man was now firmly poised on the fence. Without being committed in any way whatsoever he was now ready to jump to either side. Never underestimate the adaptability of a Croley, Justin told himself.

Gus had loaded his feed on the wagon. It was a pitifully small load, and his horses were gaunt.

"Business proposition, Gus," Justin called up to him. "Short trip down Cannon Road, light work, big pay."

"O.K.," Gus said disconsolately. Justin climbed up and Gus flapped his reins on the horses' backs. The wagon creaked down Cannon Road toward the gravel pit.

"I should have warned you," Gus said bitterly. "You're taking a chance being seen with me. I'm under suspicion as a dangerous conspirator—to be exact, a rootless Zionist cosmopolitan. The MVD came around last week. They searched the house. They took our Menorah, the Sabbath candlestick I haven't lit since Pop died. And in the attic they found the

real evidence. A bunch of mildewed haggadas,
Passover prayer-books I haven't used for
twenty years. And Granpa's Talmud in forty
little volumes of Hebrew and Aramaic which I
can't read. That makes me a rootless-
internationalist-cosmopolitan-cryptofascist-
Zionist conspirator. They warned me to keep
my nose clean. I guess they'll be back one of
these days when they haven't got anything
better to do and haul us away." He lapsed into
silence.

"Stop at Mrs. Sprenger's," Justin said.

The birdlike old lady read the note in
terror, whispered to herself, "I wish I didn't
have to," and showed them to the cistern in
the back yard. The two of them levered its
concrete slab cover aside. There was a ladder
and the cistern was stacked with provisions.

"Please," Mrs. Sprenger begged them,
"please don't take more than the note says. He
thinks I take the things myself but I wouldn't
do anything like that. Please don't make a
mistake in counting."

They carried up the food and loaded the
wagon, hiding it under the original load of
fodder.

"Christmas Eve," Justin said to Mrs.
Sprenger. And gave her a penny.

"Thank you," she said faintly.

Driving away, Feinblatt asked, "What's this
Christmas Eve-and-penny-routine, Billy?"

"Just a habit I have."

"You didn't have it a month ago. Where've
you been? You look different. You lost some
weight, but your whole face looks different."

"I had some teeth pulled."

"I see; that would do it. Billy, stop me if I'm going off side, but did you have your teeth pulled like, say, the Laceys down at Four Corners?"

"That's the way."

They were heading up Oak Hill Road by then and Justin was debating furiously with himself. He had to start somewhere, he had to start with someone. There'd never be a better starting place than strong, steady, bitter Gus Feinblatt. But he didn't want to; he didn't dare. He was learning the difference between trusting only yourself and trusting others. It was an agonizing difference.

Stalling deliberately, he asked, "What'll you have for your share of the loot?"

"I don't care. Some of the beans and flour, I suppose. We're sick of potatoes. Lord, what a winter this is going to be! I'm lucky to have Tony and Phony here; they can haul wood so I can spend my time bucking and splitting. I guess we'll make out if we close most of the house and if we can get another grate for the stove. The old one's about burned through. They aren't supposed to go fifteen years without a replacement."

"Turn right," Justin said when they reached the fork that led on the left to his place and on the right to Prospect Hill.

"What for, Billy?"

"There's something I want to show you. And something I want to ask you. Look, you rootless Zionist, how'd you like to join a real conspiracy?"

The horribly risky job of local recruiting had begun.

BOOK 4

CHAPTER NINETEEN

NOVEMBER 18 . . .

The farmer lay trembling with cold on the concrete basement floor of the Chiunga Junior High cellar.

"To your feet, please," the bored lieutenant said. The farmer tried to get up but his knees betrayed him. He collapsed again and whispered from the floor: "I told you I don't know what you're talking about, mister. I told you I just got in the habit because everybody was doing it and I didn't mean anything."

"To your feet, please," said the lieutenant. "Now sit on the stool again." He took a deep breath and roared in the exhausted man's face: "Do you think I'm a child to be taken in by fairy stories? The prisoner is lying! The prisoner knows very well that the greeting 'Christmas Eve' with the passing of a coin is a symbol of defiance!" He turned down the dazzling light that reddened the farmer's eyes and equally turned down his voice to a murmur. "You see, Mr. Firstman, we know the truth. Why are you keeping us awake with this stubbornness? You could be in bed now if you'd just said an hour ago that it's merely a token of resistance, a sort of game, merely. What do you say, Mr. Firstman; will you be a sport and let us all get some sleep?"

"All right," the farmer screamed. "All right, I guess maybe it was. I guess we got a kick out of it, it was like a password, something you Reds didn't know anything about. Call it anything you want to!"

This took the light down another notch. The lieutenant offered him a cigarette and a light and cooed: "Please, Mr. Firstman, what we want is not the point. We hope you'll help because whoever planted this dangerous seed wishes you and your friends no good. You're in trouble now in a way, but it's not your fault; the blame lies with whoever began this silly business. We only want you to help us find him, and certainly you don't owe him any friendship the way he's landed you here."

Firstman swayed on the stool after two deep drags at his cigarette. "I don't know who started it," he said stubbornly. "Like I said, everybody started to say it and pass pennies around but that's all I——"

The lieutenant plucked the cigarette from his lips and snarled: "There is no need to lie to us, prisoner." And again the light blazed into his red-rimmed eyes.

Two hours later he signed the confession and tumbled into his cot, snoring.

The lieutenant studied the document with a look of deep disgust; the captain to whom he reported came in and caught him scowling.

"And what's wrong, Sergei Ivanovtich?"

"Nothing, Pavel Gregorievitch. Also everything. Farmer Firstman had signed an admission of his guilt. In principle, so he should have; his attitude was contumacious and it was clear to me that even if he has not so far engaged in wrecking, he certainly would when the occasion presented itself."

"What about 'Christmas Eve,' Sergei Ivanovitch?" the captain asked, beginning to set up the chessmen for their game.

The lieutenant's lips went tight. 'Christmas Eve' was the captain's discovery, and on the strength of it the captain hoped to be a major soon. "It seems to mean 'Pie in the sky,' Pavel Gregorievitch. If you know the phrase?"

"Approximately the same as *Nietchevo*," the captain sighed. "I feared as much." He moved pawn to king four.

Immensely relieved, the lieutenant sat down and played the queen's pawn gambit. "Administrative disposal?" he asked.

Pawn took pawn. The captain nodded yes.

The lieutenant pursued two trains of thought simultaneously. One concerned the "administrative disposal" of farmer Firstman: it would be his job to administratively dispose of him with a pistol bullet in the back of the neck; he was wondering which pistol to use. His cherished Colt .45 was far too heavy for the job—the other concerned the margin by which he should lose the chess game to the captain.

The captain said abruptly: "We should sweat a few more of these 'Christmas Eve' sayers, Sergei Ivanovitch, but I will understand if results are negative. One cannot be right every time."

The lieutenant suppressed a smile. The captain felt self-pity, and his course was now clear. It was his duty to be roundly trounced in a dozen moves.

NOVEMBER 20, temperatures seasonably cold with snow flurries over the Northeast and light variable winds.

The proclamation left by the corporal in the jeep said the indigenous population was ordered to discontinue the faddish, slangy salutation "Christmas Eve" forthwith. For the said phrase could be substituted any one of the following traditional cultural salutations and farewells in the following list:

Ah, good day sir (or madame)!

How are crops, (first name of person addressed)? And more. Mr. Croley looked it over word by word in his empty store, then slowly tacked it to his bulletin board and waited.

Lank old Mark Tryon came in after a while and asked: "Got any white bread?"

Mr. Croley took a huge loaf of dark rye bread from its screened box in answer to that.

"Cut me off two pounds," Tryon said. "I s'pose you couldn't slice it for me?"

Mr. Croley shook his head once and measured carefully to cut off two pounds. Tryon read the placard meanwhile. He turned from it, dead pan, to pick up his chunk of bread and put down his dollar.

"Christmas Eve," Mr. Croley said, shoving back a penny change at him.

Tryon blinked, said furtively, "Christmas Eve," glanced at the placard, and scuttled out with the bread under his arm.

Mr. Croley looked after him for a moment and then turned to check through the credit books on the widespread rack. He worked through the As, noting who was over five dollars, who over ten, who over fifteen. Sir or madame! he snorted to himself silently.

NOVEMBER 23.

Stan Potocki and his wife were out in the crisp cold butchering hogs. A huge fire roared and stank, for as they boned the meat they threw bones and gristle onto the blazing chunks. It was a funny way to butcher. Stan sawed and sliced, his wife dragged cuts away to hang in the barn and between times kept herself busy digging in a row of barrels. When she finished, the barrels would be flush with the ground, filled with brine and pork, covered with the winter woodpile.

Mrs. Potocki leaned on her shovel for a moment, stamping her feet in the powdery snow. "Mrs. Winant didn't say anything when

I met her," she said.

"Henry Winant's yellow," Potocki grunted. "Killing ten sheep. 'Maybe more later, Stan, but I can't tell him hog cholera got my sheep, ya know.'" He was imitating Henry Winant's nasal twang. "I told him wild dogs could just as easy kill twenty as ten, but he's yellow. Got to ace up to the Agro man anyway, why not do it for twenty sheep?" He added, "Goddamn it," whetted his butcher knife, and stuck another pig in the throat. "Hog cholera, sudden outbreak. Had to slaughter and burn 'em fast, Lieutenant, you being an Agro man know how it is with cholera. Wanna see the bones and ashes. I'll get a shovel, buried 'em right here."

"Stan," his wife said.

He stopped and patiently began to whet his butcher's knife.

"Stan, what's gonna happen on Christmas Eve?"

He said slowly: "I don't know. I wish to hell I did. Whatever happens, we'll take it as it comes."

"I guess," she said, "hiding the pork's got something to do with it?"

"I guess," he said shortly, and laid down his whetstone and tried his butcher knife on his thumb carefully.

NOVEMBER 23.

The old phenomenon of persecution, the one that persecutors never learn, was working itself out again. The Feinblatts were getting ready for dinner. In a bungling way it

was as Kosher as they could manage,
considering that they had not kept a ritual
kitchen since Gus's father died years before.

Mrs. Feinblatt was worrying over which
dish towel was which. Did the red band mean
meat dishes and the blue band mean milk
dishes, or was it vice versa? She had forgotten; she'd have to write it down somewhere.
Kosher was a nuisance, no denying it, but a
nuisance with compensations. Nowadays
when they had so little they had at least this
feeling that they were a link in a chain
through fifty centuries. . . .

Gus was finishing a report on a lost heifer.
"Condition of fence, time last seen, direction
of hoofprints . . ." It had to be turned in to the
Agro man when he made his rounds. He
washed his hands and went through the
sliding double doors to the dining room.
Before sitting down he went to the sideboard
where the cannister set stood and scooped out
half a cup of flour and a small handful of
beans. He lifted a loose floor board and
dumped them into flat cans waiting there
between the joists.

Mrs. Feinblatt complained: "You're getting
awful queer, Gus. Why do you put the stuff
away? Why ask for trouble? They shot the
Wehrweins for hoarding, didn't they? And the
heifer! Maybe you'll get away with it, but my
heart stops every time I think of the man
looking in the barn, walking over the
barrel—Gus, I was talking to Mrs. Potocki in
the store when there wasn't anybody around
and she *knows* about it. Gus, did you tell
Sam?"

"I told him, I told him," he said wearily. "He's doing the same with his hogs. And if your heart stops, your heart stops. Sit down."

She sat.

Gus put on a hat and thought. He was vaguely aware from a novel he had read once that the fifty centuries of Jewish sacred literature provided blessings for every occasion—tasting a perfect melon, seeing purple clouds at sunset, hearing that a relative had been ransomed from heathen captivity. Presumably there was one for sitting down to a thin stew of turnips and beef in the first year of a pagan conquest, but he didn't know it. He sighed and recited the only prayer he did know, the "Hear, O Israel," and they began to eat.

DECEMBER 5.

A mass of cold Canadian air had bulged through the western Great Lakes area, bringing snow mixed with freezing rain to much of the northeastern N.A.P.D.R. Hospitals were already filled to capacity with old people coughing their lives away, and they called it virus epidemic. The truth of the matter was that it was cold and starvation.

Betsy Cardew, red-eyed and dog-tired from last night's Young Communist League meeting and the subsequent hours of volunteer work unloading at the freight yards, made her first stop of the day at the Chiunga County Country Club that was. The MVD Agro detachment had plowed it up for an experimental station.

She blinked at a new sign nailed to the archway over the driveway. It said:

"Collective Farm 'Pride of Susquehanna' (EXP CC 001)" in ugly, Russian-looking letters. She drove under it to the administration building, noting on the way other strange things going on at what used to be the first tee. Red Army trucks were arriving. Tents were being erected. Bewildered farm-looking couples were being unloaded from the trucks and guided to the tents. There was a kitchen tent with fat cooks boiling up breakfast; a chow line of farmers was shaping up.

Lieutenant Sobilov was waiting for her at the foot of the administration building's steps as usual. He was trying to make her and simultaneously polish his English. He wore the MVD green, but as an Agro scientist was only nominally in the Ministry of Internal Affairs.

She handed the mail through the window to him. "What's going on, Lieutenant?" she asked.

Sobilov looked around first. The coast was clear. "We are setting up a pilot farm," he grinned. "We are anticipating the problems of next year."

"Problems?"

After another look around Sobilov ventured an amused laugh. "My dear girl," he assured her, "peasants are peasants, the world over. Surely it can be no secret to you that your countrymen have turned obstinate?"

She looked ashamed. "But our YCL program, 'Every Farmer a Shock Worker of the Revolution'—" she began to argue.

"Na, na, na! The time is past. There are cycles of behavior, and the secret is to anticipate them. There was first the cycle of shocked apathy, which we countered by occasional salutary executions for the good of all. There is now in effect a new cycle of sullen resistance. Your countrymen think they can—put one over, is the phrase?—on the Union of Soviet Socialist Republics."

He offered her a cigarette and lit one himself. "It is amusing. It is what happened in the Ukraine in 1933. The peasants came out of shock and decided that they would put one over. They neglected to cultivate. They butchered their livestock rather than turn in the stated amount. They raised only enough grain for themselves. How is your history? What did the great Stalin do?" He chuckled affectionately at the thought of the shrewd old man.

"I don't know," she said faintly. "We're working more on the origins and early heroes of the class struggle in North America——"

"And quite rightly. I will tell you what the great Stalin did. He waited. He smiled and waited. And then in the late fall of 1933, after months of the Ukrainian nonsense, he confiscated *all* grain and livestock. The foolish peasants died by the millions through the winter. In the spring their broken remnants were easily placed in collective farms, where an eye could be kept on them and no foolishness allowed." He dragged deeply on his cigarette and shrugged. "If your countrymen too must learn the difficult way, the Union of Soviet Socialist Republics will be a cheerful schoolteacher."

"You make it all so clear, Lieutenant," Betsy said, and Sobilov smiled proudly.

As she drove on she reflected that the Ukrainians of 1933 had neither a war plan nor a bombardment satellite.

DECEMBER 14.

The cold did not penetrate the cavern under Prospect Hill, to Mr. Sparhawk's faint regret. He thought: One really ought to be in that much communication with nature that one was aware of the seasonal cycle, the great rhythm we all echo in our small, hurried bodily tick-tocking.

He was serving stewed prunes in the cafeteria to Lieutenant Colonels Byrne and Patri, and he thought it was a good time to tell them about it.

"Sure," Byrne said, eating his stewed prunes. He was a small, dark man and Patri was a small, fair man. They had arrived separately ten days ago, Byrne the pilot comfortably in a telephone-repair truck and Patri the missile master blue with cold after a ride in an unheated freight car and Betsy's unheated sedan.

"Got any more of these prunes, pop?" Patri asked. He had gobbled his dish. He was getting a little fat, overdoing his catching up on the scanty meals when he was under cover as a moronic paint sprayer in a Detroit auto plant. Byrne, a Tuskegee graduate, had hid out as a Black Belt saloonkeeper in Memphis and had missed no meals.

Mr. Sparhawk brought seconds on prunes. "You young men," he said, "really ought to make some time for a study of Zen. Japanese archers, you know, practice Zen, and it makes them the best archers in the world. Qualitatively there's no difference between the—ah—task ahead of you and archery. The great thing is to divorce oneself from the action, not to *will*. Let the bow shoot the arrow, not the bowman. Now——"

Patri wiped his mouth and got up. "Pop," he said kindly, "we'd be in a helluva mess if we let that thing fly us instead of vicey versey."

"Amen, brother," Byrne said. "Just don't you worry, pop; we'll fly it O.K. when the time comes. The prunes were swell. I really like prunes."

Mr. Sparhawk should have done the dishes; instead he trailed them forlornly to the hangar room. There they firmly said good-by and climbed into G-suits. A whining hoist descended from the jutting crane arm of Stage 1 and they hooked on and signaled. It lifted them like two drowned trout on a line, turning and swinging a little, into the dim upper reaches of the cavern. Time for another of their interminable dry runs.

Mr. Sparhawk sighed and buttonholed Dr. Dace as the white-haired little engineer hurtled past, his arms full of schematics. Dr. Dace cursed him efficiently for thirty seconds and ordered him back to the kitchen, where he was of some use. "And furthermore," Dace snarled in conclusion, "leave my technicians alone, do you understand? There's approximately 1,300 man-hours of work left to squeeze in. We're still lacking components. We have no time for your drivel!"

Dr. Dace turned and hurtled on his way.

Mr. Sparhawk said a prayer for him and went to do the dishes.

DECEMBER 20, dark and drafty in the Wehrwein's barn at eleven-thirty. The meeting was to begin at midnight. Justin had arrived early to give Hollerith—who used to be Rawson—some bad news.

"It came over the dry wires," he said. "The ticket man got it and passed it to Betsy. She gave it to me in a fake letter. Decoded, no bomb for Chiunga County. And—you're reprimanded for requesting one."

Hollerith's face went red in the lamplight. He struggled with and gave way to the impulse to curse and rail, even in front of a civilian. "I'm supposed to make a fight," he said softly. "I'm supposed to make a fight and cover the bombardment satellite with fifty farmers, some homemade firecrackers, and a few .22s' Those fatheaded——!"

"There'll be the last-minute roundup," Justin said unsympathetically. "And at least we have trucks. And the stuff they're making in the drugstore they don't use in firecrackers."

"How's she making out with the druggists?" Hollerith snapped.

"Winkler's making thermit. He says he doesn't know how to make nitro, but the fact is he's scared to try in this weather. Farish is going to make nitro."

"Going to make?"

Justin reflected that General Hollerith had been spoiled by having neatly packaged dynamite and TNT to play with too long. "The fact sheet explained all that. It doesn't keep in the cold, General. Turns into crystals, and if one crystal gets nicked—wham. End of drugstore. Don't worry. We'll have the stuff unless they blow themselves up making it fresh, which I understand is also a distinct possibility."

A couple of men came in and headed for the lantern light. "Christmas Eve," they said.

"Christmas Eve," said Hollerith.

When the rest arrived, the barn began to grow almost comfortable with their body warmth.

Hollerith leaned forward in his gocart and began to speak. "We'll have a report later from each of you on his neighbors," he said. "Tonight I want to make absolutely sure you know what we'll be doing on Christmas Eve. We'll be forcing the Reds to eat their soup with a knife. . . ."

CHAPTER TWENTY

On Christmas Eve, December 24, 8:00 P.M., Justin was wrinkling his face against a drizzle of sleet and pounding on Croley's locked door. The town of Norton was dark.

Mr. Croley's feet eventually sounded on the stairs from his apartment above the store; the door rattled and opened. The storekeeper stood there and waited.

Justin said, "Christmas Eve," and passed him a penny.

"Christmas Eve," Croley said.

Justin took out Hollerith's army .45 and stuck it in the storekeeper's ribs. He said: "I need a steady man with a central location. Open your storeroom. I want the local people's guns and ammunition."

Croley shrugged and said, "I'm bein' forced," and walked to the storeroom. He winced when Justin ripped off the Red Army seal, but unlocked the door.

"We load these in your truck, Croley," Justin said. From upstairs came a querulous voice. "Tell her it's all right," Justin said.

Croley called back upstairs that it was all right and, moving like a rusty robot, loaded rifles and boxes of ammunition in his truck outside. He broke silence only once to say: "They'll kill you for this, Justin. Don't be crazy." Justin didn't answer.

The storekeeper's eyes widened when Justin told him he was going to drive. "Crazy," he spat. "Check point on the highway'll see us go up the hill. They'll phone the road patrol. Next thing, jeeps and armored cars all up and down the farm roads."

"Don't argue. Just drive. To the Medford place first."

Long horn-tooting brought out the Medfords. In the headlight's glare Justin handed the old man and his sixteen-year-old boy each a good 30-30 and ammunition.

"These ain't our guns, Billy, we just had little varmint rifles, and anyway what's all this——?"

"We haven't got time to sort them out," Justin lied. "Wait inside. Have a hot meal. A truck'll come by for you."

The boy said joyously: "You mean——"

"Christmas Eve," Justin said. "What did you think it meant?"

At the Lyman's place up the road Henry Lyman was nothing but trouble. First he didn't want a gun. Next he wanted his own gun, not the .22 which was all Justin thought he rated. Lastly he said he wasn't at all sure he'd come when somebody came in a truck for him; he had himself to think about. Justin told him: "Mr. Lyman, you'll be called on to fight for the United States of America tonight. If you refuse to fight, the United States has every right to shoot you for cowardice and every intention of doing so as soon as it has a free moment. Get in your house, have a hot meal, and wait for the truck."

"Crazy," Mr. Croley muttered as they drove to the next farm.

9:00 P.M., Main Street, Chiunga Center.

Betsy Cardew slipped into the drugstore by the back way. Bald young Fred Farish, R.Ph., started violently over his prescription counter when she spoke. "Got them, Fred?"

"The nitro, yes. I'm finishing the thermit. There was a surprise inspection before I closed up. Went fine. What's to inspect? Nitric acid and glycerol—standard reagents. In the trash can some rust, some dust, and some beer cans." He gave her a thin, terrified smile and went on with his work.

Cappable beer cans stood in a row on his counter. He had filled them with "rust and dust"—iron oxide and powdered aluminum. With deft druggist's fingers he was filling gelatin capsules with barium peroxide and powdered magnesium; into each capsule he slipped a trailing tail of magnesium ribbon. He finished a dozen capsules, slipped them into a dozen beer cans, and passed them to Betsy. She had a shopping bag ready for them.

"And—the other stuff?"

He took a newspaper from a shelf; beneath it was a flat box partitioned into nests padded with cotton wool. The eggs in the nests were bottles filled with something that looked like yellow oil. Nitroglycerine is readily manufacturable on a small scale out of easily available chemicals by anybody who cares to take the horrible risk of doing it.

Farish gave her his terrified smile again and said abruptly: "I'm coming along, Miss Cardew. I'll carry—them." He methodically got into his overcoat and wound a scarf around his neck and tucked the padded box under the coat. "Mustn't let them get cold," he said with a near giggle. And: "I used to pitch in the Little League, Miss Cardew. Between attacks of asthma. Maybe . . ." He trailed off.

They went out the back way, she leading with her shopping bag through the dark winter street, he following at a good distance. They were heading for the north end of town, the reservoir and pumping station.

At nine-fifteen in the garage of the satellite cavern Gus Feinblatt lifted General Hollerith out of his gocart and heaved him up in the cab of a red gravel truck. Straps were sewn into the leather seat; Hollerith buckled himself in. Feinblatt climbed up in the left and started the motor. It was the signal for fifty motors in fifty trucks driven by fifty hard-core regulars of two weeks' training to start.

Dr. Dace came running to the red gravel truck and called up to Hollerith: "Give 'em hell, General!"

Hollerith, like a good general, boomed with confidence: "The old one-two, Doc!" His eyes were haunted.

He raised his arm and dropped it; the exquisitely counterpoised trap door in the good-bad road hoisted up and a drizzle of freezing rain whispered down the tunnel. The trucks began to roll out.

At nine-thirty the two MVD guards were pacing their slow patrol before the Chiunga Center pumping station—a red brick scaled-down castle with false crenelations and two towers that looked like chess pieces. Behind it the solid wall of the reservoir.

Betsy Cardew and Fred Farish watched from the shadows. Farish's teeth were chattering. "We better not get any closer," he said. "The machine guns on the roof——"

It was about fifteen yards from the board fence where they crouched to the little castle. "They ought to be heavier," Betsy said fretfully. "You should have put them in heavy bottles or wrapped them with wire or something. The pamphlet said all that."

"I forgot," Farish said miserably. "I can go back and——"

"No," she said. "There's no time." And she wrinkled her face, trying to think, trying not to cry. The pamphlet assumed the bottles would be heavy enough for a solid throw, the pamphlet assumed the druggist would have nerves of steel and the soul of a punch card, omitting not one step of the twenty it listed. The pamphlet had to assume so, and the pamphlet was wrong. Many things would go wrong that night, Betsy suddenly realized. She stood in paralysis watching the sentries pace, realizing that every mistake would be paid for to the last penny.

"Try throwing one," she said to Farish.

He eased a small bottle from its nest and pulled off his right glove with his teeth. He went into a rusty windup and hurled the bottle.

It made a very sharp, loud noise that rocked them back and made the board fence ripple against them. It wasn't at all the dull, reverberating boom Betsy had prepared herself for but more like the crack of a gigantic whip.

There didn't seem to be a second's pause before the reaction from the pumping-station-guard detachment came. Floodlights glared out, and in the frosty air they heard clanks from the roof as the section of machine guns was full-loaded and unlimbered. The two guards shouted at each other and crouched, unslinging their tommy guns and moving right across the little plaza to the edge of shadow.

The nitro bottle had pocked up the pavement yards from the door. Total failure. The sentries, ready to fire from the hip, were almost upon the fence that sheltered them.

Farish said abruptly; "Good-by, Betsy," which was the first time the bald young man had dared call Miss Cardew from up the hill by her first name. In floodlight filtering through cracks in the fence she saw the silly, terrified grin on his face. He vaulted the fence into the light and cried, his hands up, "I surrender! I give up!"

There was a wild burst of shots from one of the startled guards; they stitched the fence not far from Betsy's head. Through a crack she saw Farish talking earnestly to the guards, his hands up high; they were marching him to the pumping station. She stayed there shivering with the cold for two minutes. If nothing happened, she'd have to make a try with her thermit . . .

But there was the whipcrack again, enormously louder this time, and the floodlights went out and fragments rained about her. One brick smashed through the fence like an artillery shell, whistling.

Perhaps, she thought, he swung one of them so they'd shoot, or perhaps he fell forward and broke the bottles next to his chest—or perhaps he repented of the whole thing, perhaps he had been frantically undressing to ease the bottles to a table somewhere and his nervous hand and the cold denotated them all.

She would never know the answer, she thought, but the results were coming thick and fast. Lights were blinking on in windows, the strident ringing of telephones had already begun. Neighbors were calling from porch to porch.

And the reservoir was cracked.

It was nothing spectacular. It was just water beginning to rill from the crack in the face, bubbling into the gutters, slopping over a little onto the sidewalks, bubbling and racing on its way through town to the storm sewers of the business section, which would convey it harmlessly into the river.

Betsy got up creakily and walked a block into the darkness. She found a big frame house where lights shone upstairs as some family—whose?—chattered about the explosion and wondered if they should call up or go out and see or what. She took a beer can from her shopping bag and snapped her lighter. The twist of magnesium ribbon trailing from the can caught suddenly and with almost explosive violence; burning metal sputtered and seared the fork of her hand. She hissed with the pain and flung the star-bright flare under the big wooden porch. She should have moved on at once. Instead she dubiously watched and wondered. The igniter caught, then slowly, the iron-aluminum reaction began. In twenty seconds the beer can melted into a puddle of orange-white brilliance that crawled into an amoeboid fashion. The porch flooring above it caught, then the porch posts, then the siding of the house.

Betsy moved on amid screams from windows. At the next block she went down an alley and lobbed a beer can against a smaller house. At the next block she laid one against the foundation of a row of shops and ignited it and walked away, not looking back. Chiunga Center was beginning to wake up screaming. The streets were filling with people wearing coats over pajamas. The fires were spreading, of course, even though the volunteer hose company had come zooming from its garage; there was no pressure at the hydrants. Fred Farish had seen to that. Betsy Cardew became one among hundreds, a dazed-looking woman wandering through blazing streets with a shopping bag in her hand, here and there stopping to do something with a can from the bag.

When she saw a wall of flame ahead of her, she knew that Mr. Hosmer, the railroad ticket man, had done his job too, working his way north with the other druggist's thermit. She headed for the post office, her face streaked with tears and soot.

By ten forty-five Justin, in Croley's truck, had met the convoy and passed over the rest of his rifles. There was almost murder done when some of the men saw Croley driving. The old storekeeper put on his accustomed contemptuous silence in the face of their threats. Justin told the men to leave him alone and they almost backed away, but it was Hollerith who acted like a general and saved Croley's life. "You men," he roared at the loudest of them, "are in the Army!" In retrospect, thought Justin, it was a silly thing to say. It was even demonstrably untrue; they were bandit terrorists according to the pre-vailing law of the land; by a generous construction of the rules of warfare, irregular partisans at the most. But somehow the word *Army* from Hollerith's mouth canceled all that . . .

So it was that Hollerith's truck and Croley's stood abreast at the intersection of the highway and the Norton road, and down the highway gleamed the light in the roadblock that used to be a truck-weighing station. They were waiting for the rest of the convoy to rendezvous, each truck with its load of hastily awakened, hastily armed farmers who knew only that it was Christmas Eve and that their neighbors were telling them: "Fight or die now."

Hollerith was twiddling the dials of a command radio set in the cab of his truck, loot from the cavern. It crackled Russian wherever he tuned it. Croley complained to Justin: "My feet're freezing. Why'n't you drive for a spell?"

"All right," Justin said, and they shifted seats. Croley stamped his feet against the floor boards and grumbled: "Damn foolishness. Get us all shot."

Justin said: "If you can't stand the suspense, get out and start running. You'll get shot that much sooner. By me."

Croley was loquacious. "Young snots," he muttered. "What I can't see is a steady man like that Rawson chargin' around. Him you call Hollerith now."

Justin repeated his suggestion.

"Don't talk foolish," Croley said testily. "Think I'm a nut? I'll go along with anybody.

Doesn't matter who."

And, Justin sensed, Croley did not realize he was degrading himself below the level of mankind to say such a thing, to be such a thing as he was. . . .

The sky lightened glaringly to the north, then subsided to a dimmer glow.

"General!" Justin yelled. He cranked down his window, reached over, and jabbed Hollerith. "Look!"

Hollerith turned from his radio, blinking, and awakened to the north sky. He whipped out a compass, took a bearing on the center of the lightness. His face broke out into a sunny grin. "Elmira!" he breathed. "Elmira! The air base and the gas depot. No gunships tonight, Billy! They got Elmira!"

They—what handful of desperately frightened men?—had got Elmira and solved General Hollerith's pressing problem of air attack. And elsewhere? Justin asked.

"The radio's pretty hot," Hollerith said, indulging the civilian situation. "Every command's yelling for Washington, but Washington doesn't come in at all. They *should* be transmitting in code," he said with a momentary frown. "It's elementary that modern guerrillas will have an RT intercept service. I'm surprised at them."

Justin begged for detail. Hollerith genially translated snatches. "Tank park in Rochester says its vehicles are out—sugar in the gas tanks. Speaking of sugar, did Gribble get off?"

"He got off,' Justin said as if to a child.

"Betsy delivered the uniform, he filled his pockets, and away he went. What else is going on?"

"Well, a smug MVD general in New Orleans says the situation's under control, 'brief and petty insurrection well in hand' —but they were supposed to get two suitcase bombs. I wonder who goofed? Never occurred to me that New Orleans would be under the MVD, but I suppose it's only natural. They're a stiff-necked people, it took old Silver Spoons Butler to handle them in the Civil War. And let's see, the Transport Overcommand is pulling rank from Pittsburgh. They want all units to furnish via their own trucks 20 per cent of their strength for immediate and vital rail, highway, and harbor repairs. And there're some Chinese coming in from the West, but I don't know the language."

"What about the satellite?" asked Justin.

The general said with elaborate detachment: "Not my baby. Couldn't say, Billy." He glanced at his watch. *"Where* are the rest of the trucks? Billy, run and take a look up Oak Hill Road, see if there're any headlights coming our way. We have to take the blockhouse sooner or later."

Justin saw no headlights.

"I guess they're held up a little," Hollerith said. "Let's go get that roadblock now."

Justin was speechless for a long moment. He said at last: "You mean—us?"

Hollerith lost his temper. "And just who in hell did you think I meant, the Fighting 69th? I mean *us*. Feinblatt and I will roll up with our

lights on. You and Croley ride in the back.
Drop off and walk the last hundred feet.
Feinblatt'll gun the motor and I'll keep 'em
busy with small talk in broken Russian. Then
you shoot 'em from the dark. Croley, you got a
rifle? Take my carbine."

"I don't trust Croley," Justin said flatly.

"Billy," said Hollerith, "I've had considerable experience with both turncoats and
reorganizing a war-disrupted area. We're
going to need Croley and we can trust him.
He'll stay bought."

Croley snorted in the dark. Justin and he
got out and climbed into the back of the other
truck.

The little raid went like clockwork. The two
Russian soldiers, gesticulating in the light,
collapsed like puppets with cut strings under
the murderous fire of Justin and Croley from
twenty feet away.

It was Justin's first personal killing. Like
most riflemen of the twentieth century he had
done his firing at two to three hundred yards,
aiming at impersonal specks which usually
dropped when he fired, giving him no clue at
all as to whether they were killed, wounded,
or taking cover. He felt sick and shaken. Not
so Croley. The old man inspected the two
Russians and said: "Dirty skunks."

"You did business with them," Justin said
faintly.

"I can do business with anybody. But you
think I *liked* them going over the books,
bothering a man all the time? Things are
going to be better if we get away from this."

It was as tepid a revolutionary manifesto, perhaps, as was ever spoken.

Hollerith was eased down from the truck and into his gocart by Feinblatt and Justin. He muscled himself into the blockhouse and called to Gus to bring the radio in and then stay outside on guard.

"Rank has its privileges," he said, gratefully turning up a kerosene heater. "And I see they had a pot of tea brewing. Croley, pour me a cup and help yourself."

Feinblatt popped in. "Headlights," he said. "It's either our boys or the whole Red Army."

"Detruck them, Billy," said Hollerith. "Get 'em into some kind of formation. Yell 'Attention' when I come out to talk."

Practically every man in the fifty trucks had gone through military training; there was little confusion. There seemed to be about two hundred gathered by scouring the hills for all males of sixteen and over. Justin got them into ranks grouped on the fifty men who had received some briefings over the past two weeks.

Hollerith's speech went like this: "Christmas Eve. It's here. I'm General Hollerith. And you, my friends, are the Army of the United States. See the sky to the west? That's Chiunga Center, burning to the ground. You heard some thunder a while ago? It wasn't thunder; it was the Susquehanna bridges being blown.

"The Red troops in the Center have got to pull up and march. Their food dumps have been burned. We've destroyed their water supply. We've cut their highway and rail lines so they have no way of getting any more. Right through here is the only way they can march.

"We have to knock out their trucks and kill their commanders. We have to leave them starving, frozen stragglers in our hills, where we can kill them on our own terms. They are a regiment—about a thousand of them. There are about two hundred of you. You have rifles and an average of two dozen rounds apiece. For you crow-shooting, deer-hunting S.O.B.s that should be plenty. Leaders, take your groups and move out."

He wheeled his gocart about and rolled into the blockhouse. Justin followed and closed the door.

The general said, not looking around, in a hoarse whisper: "But will they?"

Justin looked and said: "Sure. There they go. Whooping and yelling, too."

The general said, "They must be nuts," and turned on the radio.

At 11:30 P.M. in the vehicle of the MVD detachment in Chiunga Center the man called Gribble was doing the job he had demanded, fought, even brokenly wept for.

The park was the drill field back of the high school building, and it was in ordered confusion. The vicious incendiary fires lapped at the rim of the field, dying now as century-old houses crumbled into orange-flecked charcoal. A tide of people surged against the field also and was turned back repeatedly by soldiers who clubbed and jabbed with their rifles. Within the line of troops the MVD regiment was forming for motor convoy. Their colonel was doing the obvious, inevitable thing. Without food and water soldiers cannot live; therefore the regiment must go to food and water.

The trucks were ready and waiting. Somebody shouted something at Gribble; he said, *"Da,"* saluted, and hurried on. He was wearing a homemade imitation of the MVD green uniform. The green would never pass by daylight, nor would the linoleum imitations of leather belt and puttees, but it was not necessary for them to pass by daylight.

Gribble was looking for the field kitchen and found it. The cooks, overcoats on top of their whites, were serving one for the road to the troops; hunks of solid black bread and dippers of tea from great boilers. Against the blazing background of the school building the men filed past, one hand out for the bread, canteen cup out for the tea. There were five boilers left when Gribble found the tent; he didn't know how many had already been emptied. As he watched, the cooks came to the bottom of one boiler; they yanked it back into the tent and shoved another into place at the serving counter. As he watched, the rear fly of the tent was pulled, folded, and hurled aboard the mess truck; the tent was disintegrating from the rear under the practiced attack of the cooks. Gribble drifted among them, among the three boilers of tea in reserve, despite their warning shouts. When they were all struggling with a big side fly, he impartially sweetened the boilers of tea with white powder from his pockets.

He had morbidly asked about it and learned that the stuff was arsenious trioxide, procured from the remelt shop of Corning Glass.

He wandered off foggily. There was a spark in the fog which wanted him to run screaming to the cooks and tell them he had poisoned the good tea, that they must stop serving it to the soldiers—he saw them drain the boiler at the counter, hurl it back, and drag forward the next.

He knew by then that he was a monster. Who but a monster could do what he had done, slaying five thousand devoted scientists and engineers by the simple closing of a door? Now causing the horrible death of how many young soldiers he did not know?

He screamed and began to run away from himself, hurtling into tents, trucks, soldiers. Somebody seized him by the front of his coat and slapped his face sharply; he broke loose and ran again. Then there was a brief interlude under a flashlight during which sharp questions rang in his ears and he could answer them only by weeping.

It ended with a tremendous padded blow on the back of his neck, which was all he felt of the lieutenant's pistol bullet destroying his brain. He never knew hundreds of soldiers squirming themselves settled in the trucks were at that very moment complaining about food as soldiers always do; they said their tea was too sweet.

At eleven-thirty Justin was establishing the
first roadblock in the path of the MVD motor
convoy, five miles east on the highway from
Chiunga Center. Heading a commando of five
untrained men and boys whom he didn't
know, he steered his truck athwart the two-
lane concrete strip and ordered them out. The
six of them grunted and strained in the icy
night air rocking the truck on its springs,
trying to tip it over. It swayed farther and
farther with each shove; on the twentieth it
almost heeled but then crashed back solidly
on its four wheels while the six men stood
panting and beaten.

"Lights," said a sixteen-year-old boy named
Sheppard. The aura of headlights was just
becoming visible over a rise to the east. They
scrambled for the roadside and into the brush
about ten yards.

"Remember what I told you," Justin
whispered. "Don't look at their headlights at
all. Officers first. When they come after us,
fall back and snipe the main body of the
convoy."

"Yeah," the Sheppard boy whispered,
fascinated.

The aura of light became beams and then
blazing pairs of eyes. *"Don't look,"* said
Justin.

The lights snapped out fast when they
picked up the truck. The advance guard—
it was six jeeps—knew a roadblock wasn't a
roadblock unless it was defended. By

starlight and a little moon the commando saw MVD men scrambling out and flattening on the road. One soldier talked loudly into a radio before getting out. Justin discovered that he couldn't tell insignia.

"Forget what I said about officers," he said. "Fire and fall back, then west."

He aimed into a clump of three men who were belly down on the road, peering off the roadside and whispering. At least one had to be an officer or noncom giving orders. He fired six shots from his carbine; at the range he couldn't miss. All three men floundered and yelled.

Around him blazed the rifles of his men, firing at what he didn't know.

A command in Russian from the road and the MVD men uncertainly began to fire in their general direction; somebody had seen muzzle flash from one of the old guns. The bullets whistled above them (people fire high in the dark) except for one that stopped with a meaty chunk in young Sheppard's head. Justin scooped up the boy's varmint rifle and box of ammunition. "Fall back," he said.

They clustered tight behind him, trampling and talking until he cursed them. He headed right, guiding on glimpses of the white road in starlight seen through ragged trees until there were the brighter lights of the convoy to guide them. They had stopped on radio word from the point, but had not yet blacked out. Justin fell farther back into the woods, saw the black hump of a little rise, and crawled up it on his belly.

"Don't fire," he whispered. "Something's going on."

One truck was emptying; that would be a platoon sent forward to reinforce the point and get the truck off the road. In the headlights half the platoon seemed to be drunk; they were lurching and holding their stomachs. Justin could barely make out features when they swayed across a headlight's beam. They were in agony, and Justin knew what it meant. Gribble had made it with his white arsenic. Good-by, Gribble, insurance executive, security officer, hatchet man, poisoner, child of self-torment. . . .

Some men were hanging from the other trucks, vomiting.

"Fire off your rounds," Justin said. "Officers and noncoms. Then we get out of here and back to the roadblock." They spread out along the rise and began to squeeze off careful shots. Justin fired four times at a shouting, waving captain and missed all four times. Grinding his teeth, he hurled his carbine aside and blazed away wildly with young Sheppard's .22; just before the convoy lights went out he dropped his man.

They had lost their night vision watching the convoy; they stumbled and crashed their way east along the roadside until it slowly returned. They heard shots behind them and then machine-gun fire. It was probably another commando sniping the convoy from its left flank and getting worse than it gave.

They hugged the roadside, passing other roadblock trucks, some successfully toppled, on their way back to the weighing-station commando post. ("Christmas Eve" was the watchword.)

Justin went in and told Hollerith: "We lost one man and wasted a lot of ammunition but our truck stopped them temporarily five miles out of town. Gribble got through with his sugar; my guess is one man in four affected."

"Good," Hollerith said. "Have some tea."

Justin gulped a tin cup of scalding tea from the top of the kerosene heater. "What about the satellite?" he asked.

Hollerith said tightly: "One man said he believes he saw it take off at eleven forty-five."

Justin's heart leaped. "Then—then we've—"

"Then we don't know, Justin. The satellite's invisible. Its exhaust isn't. If our man saw it, do you suppose no one else did?"

Justin's heart stopped short. "I don't understand!" he cried. "If the Reds can spot it, what's the good of it?"

"That's what we find out a little later on. Maybe the Red spy satellites were all knocked out when ours were. Maybe they won't believe what they see. Maybe anything you damn please, but at least if got off the ground—also maybe. I didn't see it. I was busy at the time."

One of the trained men came in, wild-eyed and bleeding from a crudely wrapped wound of his left hand. "Hi, Rawson," he said. General Hollerith looked annoyed. "We got there second," the man said. "Some other gang was banging away and they blacked out.

They fired at us a lot and a machine gun killed both my brothers. With the same burst."

"What did you see?" Hollerith urged gently.

The man rambled: "They looked sick, lots of them. They unloaded a lot of their men and their medics with the bands and a lot of blankets. Left 'em right there in the road and the trucks moved on up with their lights out and soldiers out beating the bushes on each side of the road."

"That's fine," Hollerith said quietly. "About five miles an hour in low gear?"

"That'd be about right," the man said. "Did I tell you they killed James and Henry? My brothers."

Hollerith said: "Have some tea, Hanson. Take it outside with you." He nodded to Justin, who put a mug of tea in the man's unwounded hand and gently steered him from the little house. Hanson sat down and began to cough. Justin walked away when the coughs turned into sobs.

There were headlights coming down Oak Hill Road off the highway. The car made the turn and headed for the command post, stopping a hundred feet away. Justin didn't know how he knew, but he was sure it was Betsy. She was soot-stained and bedraggled and silent; she carried a bulging shopping bag. He took her in to Hollerith. She laid down the shopping bag carefully and began to unpack it on the general's table. She said: "Winkler had a sudden rush of courage. He met me at the post office garage with this stuff. Extra thermit he turned out and some nitro in flat bottles."

"How's the Center?" snapped Hollerith.

"Still burning, I guess," she said listlessly. "What about the satellite?"

Hollerith said in a low, venomous voice: "To hell with the satellite. How am I supposed to know about the satellite? Maybe it's crashed in Nebraska or the Atlantic by now. Maybe it never got up. Maybe it's on its way into the sun. I'm no mind reader, Miss Cardew, so kindly shut up about the satellite."

Stan Potocki came in and looked apologetic. "Gus got killed," he said. "One of their patrols tossed grenades when they heard us. Blown in half—but I guess you want a report. The convoy is proceeding east on the highway under blackout with flank patrols. They are stopping from time to time to move our road-blocks. They are averaging maybe three miles an hour, I figure, because their walking patrols aren't having any trouble keeping up. I don't know whether our sniping's having any real effect on them except to kill a few of their people. They're going to get through, General."

"Thanks, Potocki," Hollerith said. "We've got some stuff here for you to lay in their path. It's nitroglycerine; handle with care. Mass all these together; maybe we can crater the road. Put it where one of our roadblock trucks'll run over it when they move it. And send in anybody outside who wants a job."

Two exhausted men came in; one saluted shame-facedly. Hollerith gave him the thermit bombs. "Take these to the top of the old Lehigh cut. They're incendiaries; you just light them. Got matches? Here, take mine. You ought to get some fine results from dropping them into open personnel trucks."

The man grinned, took the shopping bag, and left. "Young Joe Firstman. They killed his father a few days ago," he told Justin in an aside. To the other man he said: "Take those dinner plates out of that cabinet there. Yes, that's what I said! I want you to lay 'em face down in the road between Truck Six and Truck Seven."

"Aw," the man said incredulously.

"Listen," Hollerith said patiently. "I mean what I say. It'll cost them ten minutes and thirty men if our shooting is any good. They'll see them, they'll know they're plates, and still won't dare roll over them until their bomb-disposal men have come up and removed them. Is that clear?"

"I guess so," the man said doubtfully, and took the plates and went out.

"Five to one he goofs off," said Hollerith, looking after him dismally.

Mr. Sparhawk entered and came to a heel-clicking, palm-out British salute before Hollerith. "Sir," he said, "I have the honor to report that the satellite vessel was launched at 11:45 hours. Dr. Dace said that all appeared to be well on radar track. He instructed me to take a recon car and report."

"Thank you," Hollerith said. "Now everybody be quiet and let me think. Very shortly the Reds will decide they won't be made to eat

soup with a knife. They'll pull in their flank
guards, turn on their lights, and go barreling
through, taking their losses and consoling
themselves with thoughts of coming back and
killing us bandit terrorists an inch at a time. I
think they'll reach the decision at about oh-
oh-one-five. Justin, sound the recall, check the
wind, and give 'em gas."

Justin went outside, Betsy trailing after,
and cranked a siren on a truck loaded with
long cylinders from the satellite cavern.
"Betsy," he said, "this stuff is chlorine. I'm
going to drive east to the cut about three
miles from here. If the wind is right, I open
the valves for the Red convoy to run into a
cloud of the stuff. Will you tail me in your car
so I can hop in and get back here? By then the
command post will be dismantled and we'll
all be heading for high ground."

"All right," she said.

On Christmas morning at 12:30 A.M. General
Hollerith, Justin, Betsy, Mr. Croley, and Mr.
Sparhawk were in Sparhawk's recon car on
the ridge road with a view of the chlorine-
filled cut below.

"I was right," Hollerith said abstractedly.
"Here they come."

With headlights on the convoy was rolling
eastward at fair speed. Into the chlorine.

It was easy to imagine the hellish confusion
below. Headlight beams angled crazily as
drivers found themselves retching over their
wheels; in the trucks dazed soldiers must
have been scratching wildly under useful
blankets, mess gear, and overcoats for long-

forgotten gas masks. Some trucks butted into the walls of the cut. But slowly, slowly, the convoy reformed and limped on.

Hollerith was swearing under his breath. At last he said: "We didn't smash them locally." The radio in the recon car squawked in Chinese. "What's happened elsewhere we don't know yet. Compared to what I privately expected, it's been a howling success. If it could be followed up—but of course it can't be followed up. It was a one-punch affair. If the Reds had broken and scattered, it would have been . . ." He sighed. "But they're going to make it through to Rochester or Syracuse or wherever they're headed, and they'll regroup and . . ." He sighed again.

The radio switched from Chinese to Russian. The general's head snapped sharply toward the speaker and he said at last: "That was it. English next."

The radio said: "M.S. One to Earth. To the peoples of Russia and China. This is Military Satellite One of the United States Armed Forces Broadcasting via drone retransmitter. You have already discovered we cannot be observed. The drone can, while it is transmitting, but it is expendable; we have plenty more drones. And plenty of bombs. Accordingly, we hereby deliver the following ultimatum: Your occupation troops in North America must surrender within twenty-four hours. Repatriation of North American prisoners of war must begin within twenty-four hours. Unless these demands are met, the cities of Moscow and Peiping will be destroyed. If the demands are still not met within a further twenty-four hours, the cities of Leningrad and Hong Kong will be destroyed. If our demands are not met, we shall continue destroying Russian and Chinese cities at twenty-four-intervals until our stock of hydrogen weapons is exhausted. We shall then drop bombs capable of generating fission-product clouds upstream from the land masses of Russia and China which will wipe out all life in those areas. Peoples of Russia and China, make your voices heard while you can. It is your rulers alone who condemn you to certain death if they refuse our ultimatum."

The voice switched to Chinese again.

They stood in utter silence through a complete replay of the ultimatum in three languages. The general reached out at last and gently turned a switch and the radio fell silent. "That will do it," he said softly. "Feng and Novikov are stubborn, but when their cities begin to go, they'll come around—or be deposed by rulers who will come around."

"So it's all over," Betsy said wonderingly.

Hollerith's face was a mixture of bitterness and defiant pride. "No," he said. "We've got to start work on people immediately. They mustn't make *that* mistake, not ever. It isn't over and it'll never be over. What happens next is the Reds build a ghost bombardment satellite of their own—secretly, in spite of all the controls we clamp on them. It'll take them a few years. We use those years to build a better satellite that'll shoot them out of the sky anyway, maybe detecting gamma rays

—but they'll know that so theirs will be a jump ahead. Don't ever think it'll be over. There's always going to be work for people like me."

Sparhawk was down on his knees talking quietly: "Deliver me, O Lord, from the evil men, preserve me from the violent men which imagine wickedness in their hearts; continually are they gathered together for war . . ."

Justin noted that he was praying not to Annie Besant or the Zen patriarchs or to Vishu but to the God of his Sunday school and regimental worship. He wondered if somehow the past night had burned away a great deal of wordy nonsense from Mr. Sparhawk's brain and left the pure metal of worship.

"Croley," General Hollerith was saying, "this is where you come in. We now have hell's own problem of supply and housing. I suppose I'm the government hereabouts now, but I'm going to be a very busy man making the Reds decent prisoners of war, keeping them from turning into bandits and scavengers. I'm going to delegate food supply to you; you know rationing procedures from your business and you know where and who the jobbers and wholesalers are. Think you can handle it?"

"Might," said Croley.

"Billy," the general said, "you're a good man and we need you. You can be my right arm in this prisoner-of-war roundup deal or you can work with Croley here getting the food lines in operation again—What's the matter?"

Billy Justin, once a commercial artist,

thirty-eight years old, a pensioned veteran of Korea, four years a dairy farmer and one year a conspirator, trigger man of the weapon that held Earth hostage, newly and suddenly seeker of God, said over his shoulder to Hollerith, "Nothing's the matter, General. I just decided I couldn't work with you or Croley. No offense, I hope."

He knelt beside Mr. Sparhawk, who was praying, "Put up again thy sword into his place for they that take the sword shall perish from the sword. Ye lust and have not; ye kill and desire to have, and cannot obtain; ye fight and war because ye ask not . . ."

They stared at Billy Justin, but after a while Betsy came and joined him.

Some thirty thousand books are published each year—about a thousand of them science fiction—and each new flood does its best to obliterate all the tides before it. Since libraries and book stores have finite space on their racks, it is not always easy to find works, even masterworks, of a writer who died a generation ago.

Currently in print, however, is *The Best of C. M. Kornbluth* (Ballantine Books), which contains nearly half of Cyril Kornbluth's shorter science-fiction stories, and almost all of his very best. Also in print are a number of books Kornbluth and I wrote in collaboration. Four are science-fiction novels: *The Space Merchants* (Ballantine), and *Gladiator-at-Law*, *Wolfbane* and *Search the Sky* (Bantam Books). Two others are collections of our shorter science-fiction stories: *Critical Mass* and *Before the Universe* (Bantam).

After that the task gets harder. There are four other science-fiction novels in the Kornbluth canon. *Takeoff* and *The Syndic* were written by Kornbluth alone; *Outpost Mars* and *Gunner Cade* in collaboration with Judith Merril. None of these is currently available, and that is a very great pity.

As far as I know, no one has yet prepared an exhaustive bibliography of Kornbluth's work. There are two main problems in doing this. One lay in his extensive use of pseudonyms in the first stage of his writing, from 1939 to around 1942, when Cyril was still in his teens: S. D. Gottesman, Cecil Corwin, Walter C. Davies, Paul Dennis Lavond, Ivar Towers and heaven knows how many others. The other was caused by the Futurian habit of collaboration in those years; some of the stories were Cyril's alone, many written jointly with Robert A. W. Lowndes, Dirk Wylie, Donald A. Wollheim, John B. Michel and myself (and with others still!) Since no exegesis was ever published, the precise authorship of many of those stories can be found only by consulting the memories of the parties involved . . . and sometimes they have forgotten.

All this is Kornbluth's science fiction (or, rarely, fantasy). In the greatest period of his writing, from 1949 until his death in 1958, he also wrote seven or eight novels that were not sf: *The Naked Storm, Half, Man of Cold Rages* and others of his own, and *Presidential Year, A Town is Drowning* and *Sorority House* in collaboration with me. None of these is currently in print, either, though *Man of Cold Rages*, at least, is a first-rate work. At the time of his death he had contracted for two other novels, neither of them science fiction. *The Crater* was a novel about an episode in the Civil War. It was an ambitious task. Cyril had done a great deal of research for it, and even completed a first draft. Unfortunately, the draft is bare bones of fact and plot, without the characterization and the brilliant use of words that marked Kornbluth's work; it has never been published. The other novel, untitled, was to have been a historical work about St. Dacius. Cyril told me that he thought it would be the book on which he would be willing to rest his reputation. But, if he ever put any part of it on paper, it did not turn up among his effects after the snowy morning in early spring when he shoveled out his driveway, ran to catch a train and died on the station platform as his overstrained heart finally gave out.

—Frederik Pohl

THE BEST IN SCIENCE FICTION

Buy them at your local bookstore or use this handy coupon:
Clip and mail this page with your order

TOR BOOKS—Reader Service Dept.
49 W. 24 Street, New York, N.Y. 10010

Please send me the book(s) I have checked above. I am enclosing
$_____ (please add $1.00 to cover postage and handling).
Send check or money order only—no cash or C.O.D.'s.

Mr./Mrs./Miss _____

Address _____

City _____ State/Zip _____

Please allow six weeks for delivery. Prices subject to change without
notice.